TWENTIETH CENTURY AMERICAN SHORT STORIES

JEAN A. McCONOCHIE

TWENTIETH CENTURY AMERICAN SHORT STORIES

COLLIER MACMILLAN INTERNATIONAL
A Division of Macmillan Publishing Co., Inc.
New York

COLLIER MACMILLAN PUBLISHERS
London

Library of Congress Catalog Card Number: 75–5236
Philippines Copyright 1975
by Collier Macmillan International
A Division of Macmillan Publishing Co., Inc.

Cover Design by Richard Nebiola

Collier Macmillan International
A Division of Macmillan Publishing Co., Inc.
866 Third Avenue, New York, N.Y. 10022
Collier Macmillan Canada, Ltd.

Printed in the United States of America
20 19 18 17 16 15 14 13 12

CREDITS AND ACKNOWLEDGMENTS
"The Chaser" Copyright 1940 by John Collier,
Copyright renewed 1968 by the author. Reprinted by
permission of Harold Matson Company, Inc.

"The Use of Force" from THE FARMERS' DAUGHTER by
William Carlos Williams. Copyright 1938 by
William Carlos Williams. Reprinted by permission
of New Directions Publishing Corporation.

"The Killers" (copyright 1927 Charles Scribner's
Sons, renewal © 1955) by Ernest Hemingway from
MEN WITHOUT WOMEN is reprinted by permission
of Charles Scribner's Sons, and the Executors
of the Ernest Hemingway Estate.

"The Unicorn in the Garden" Copyright © 1940
James Thurber, Copyright © 1968 Helen Thurber,
from FABLES FOR OUR TIME, published by Harper and
Row, New York, and from VINTAGE THURBER by James
Thurber copyright © 1963 Hamish Hamilton, London.
Originally printed in *The New Yorker*. Reprinted by permission
of Mrs. James Thurber and the publishers.

Dedication

To Dr. Vivian Horn, who guided some of my first efforts as a teacher with infinite tact, patience and gentleness.

Contents

Preface

The nine stories in this volume are representative of the best Ameri
can short stories published in the present century. Some are humor
ous, others are serious. Some have a rural setting, others are urban
or suburban. All explore universal questions in the context of
American cultural patterns. The ultimate choice of stories was based
on the criteria of recognized literary quality, brevity, and cultural
and linguistic accessibility to non-native speakers of American
English.

The book was conceived as a text for advanced students of English
as a second or foreign language. However, the stories are sufficiently
challenging to be appropriate for native speakers in a junior college
freshman English course. The stories are complete and unsimplified;
three—"The Killers," "The Lottery," and "The Secret Life of
Walter Mitty"—have each been divided into two parts to make them
a manageable length for a single assignment. The twelve chapters,
each consisting of a story and accompanying materials, are intended
for use in one semester of twelve to fifteen weeks.

The GLOSSARY accompanying each story includes (1) words or
idioms which even advanced students of English as a second or
foreign language would be unlikely to know, e.g. *cerulean* in "The
Orphaned Swimming Pool"; (2) any word used in one of its less-
common meanings, e.g. *browsing* in "The Unicorn in the Garden";
(3) regional or non-standard variants of American English, e.g. *Let's
don't.* in "Love"; (4) slang or argot, e.g. *booby* in "The Unicorn
in the Garden". In addition, (5) items unique to American culture
such as brand names (e.g. *Squibb's* in "The Secret Life of Walter
Mitty"), geographic references (e.g. *Pell Street* in "The Chaser")
and holidays (e.g. *Halloween* in "The Lottery") are explained in
terms of their significance in the story.

Words or expressions listed in the Glossary are marked with an
asterisk (*). Words are glossed on their first appearance; the gloss
is not repeated if the word recurs in a subsequent story. Nouns are
defined in their singular form; verbs are defined in the tense in which
they occur, to avoid the problem of finding the proper headword for

an irregular verb. Those familiar with *The Advanced Learner's Dictionary** will recognize the use of a tilde (~) to signal the place of a headword in an example phrase, e.g. *"just as gentle—* ~ as can be " in "The Killers."

Detailed COMPREHENSION AND DISCUSSION QUESTIONS follow each story. They are intended, first, to guide the student in his reading and, in some cases, to clarify a difficult point in the story. It may, indeed, be wise for students to read through the questions *before* reading a story for the first time. The second use of the questions is to aid the teacher in guiding class discussion. Questions intended for this latter function are starred (*); they are, for the most part, those which require the student to develop his skills in inference and interpretation. Individual teachers will, of course, want to base their selection of questions for class discussion on the linguistic and cultural sophistication of their students.

The EXERCISES following each story focus on vocabulary, grammar and syntax. They are based directly on the texts, both to enhance the reader's understanding of what he has just read and to help him assimilate new words and grammatical constructions for his own use. All of the exercises may be done orally in class and/or assigned as written homework. Again, the choice and use of the exercises will depend on the linguistic needs of a given class. Widely varied in format, the exercises range in difficulty from choosing synonyms to identifying imagery and stylistic nuances.

For three stories—"The Chaser," "The Killers," and "The Secret Life of Walter Mitty"—the final exercise is a classroom dramatization of the text. These dramatizations provide students an opportunity to practice a wide range of styles in conversational English and also bring out aspects of the story which may not have been apparent in silent reading.

Following each story are TOPICS FOR DISCUSSION AND COMPOSITION. Those dealing with plot, characterization or style are an extension of the "Comprehension and Discussion Questions." That is, their purpose is to guide the student to a deeper understanding and appreciation of the story. Other topics,

* A. S. Hornby, E. V. Gatenby, H. Wakefield, *The Oxford Advanced Learner's Dictionary of Current English*, New Third Edition. London: Oxford University Press, 1974.

which call for free discussion or writing on a theme suggested by the story, are intended to stimulate the students to relate what they have read to their own ideas and experiences.

The BIOGRAPHICAL NOTES ON THE AUTHORS AND SUGGESTIONS FOR FURTHER READING at the end of the text are there for the curious reader.

In preparing these materials, I have benefited greatly from the encouragement and suggestions of both students and colleagues. Among the latter, Gloria Gallingane and Pamela Breyer have been exceptionally generous. I am also thankful to Eleanor Baker, Jeanne Constantin and Chick and Nelly Mitchell for their help.

TWENTIETH CENTURY AMERICAN SHORT STORIES

JOHN COLLIER

The *Chaser

Alan Austen, as nervous as a *kitten, went up certain dark and creaky stairs in the neighborhood of *Pell Street, and *peered about for a long time on the dim *landing before he found the name he wanted written obscurely on one of the doors.

He pushed open this door, as he *had been told to do, and found himself in a tiny room, which contained no furniture but a plain kitchen table, a *rocking-chair, and an ordinary chair. On one of the dirty *buff-colored walls were a couple of shelves, containing in all perhaps a dozen bottles and jars.

An old man sat in the rocking-chair, reading a newspaper. Alan, without a word, handed him the card he had been given. "Sit down, Mr Austen," said the old man very politely. "I am glad to make your acquaintance."

"Is it true," asked Alan, "that you have a certain mixture that has—er—quite extraordinary effects?"

"My dear sir," replied the old man, "my stock in trade is not very large—I don't deal in *laxatives and *teething mixtures—but such as it is, it is varied. I think nothing I sell has effects which could be precisely described as ordinary."

"Well, the fact is— " began Alan.

"Here, for example," interrupted the old man, reaching for a bottle from the shelf. "Here is a liquid as colorless as water, almost tasteless, quite *imperceptible in coffee, milk, wine, or any other beverage. It is also quite imperceptible to any known method of *autopsy."

"Do you mean it is a poison?" cried Alan, very much horrified.

"Call it a glove-cleaner if you like," said the old man indifferently. "Maybe it will clean gloves. I have never tried. One might call it a life-cleaner. Lives need cleaning sometimes."

"I want nothing of that sort," said Alan.

"Probably it is just as well," said the old man.

"Do you know the price of this? For one *teaspoonful, which is sufficient, I ask *five thousand dollars. Never less. Not a penny less."

1

"I hope all your mixtures are not as expensive," said Alan *apprehensively.

"Oh dear, no," said the old man. "It would be no good charging that sort of price for a love *potion, for example. Young people who need a love potion very seldom have five thousand dollars. Otherwise they would not need a love potion."

"I am glad to hear that," said Alan.

"I look at it like this," said the old man. " *Please a customer with one article, and he will come back when he needs another. Even if it *is* more *costly. He will save up for it, if necessary."

"So," said Alan, "do you really sell love potions?"

"If I did not sell love potions," said the old man, reaching for another bottle, "I should not have mentioned the other matter to you. It is only whan one is in a position to oblige that one can afford to be so confidential."

"And these potions," said Alan. "They are not just—just—*er——."

"Oh, no," said the old man. "Their effects are permanent, and extend far beyond casual impulse. But they include it. *Bountifully, insistently. Everlastingly."

"Dear me!" said Alan, attempting a look of scientific detachment. "How very interesting!"

"But consider the spiritual side," said the old man.

"I do indeed," said Alan.

"For indifference," said the old man, "they substitute devotion. For scorn, adoration. Give one tiny measure of this to the young lady—its flavor is imperceptible in orange juice, soup, or cocktails—and however gay and *giddy she is, she will change altogether. She will want nothing but solitude, and you."

"I can hardly believe it," said Alan. "She is so fond of parties."

"She will not like them anymore," said the old man. "She will be afraid of the pretty girls you may meet."

"She will actually be jealous?" cried Alan in a *rapture. "Of me?"

"Yes, she will want to be everything to you."

"She is already. Only she doesn't care about it."

"She will, when she has taken this. She will care intensely. You will be her *sole interest in life."

"Wonderful!" cried Alan.

"She will want to know all you do," said the old man. "All that has happened to you during the day. Every word of it. She will want to know what you are thinking about, why you smile suddenly, why you are looking sad."

"That is love!" cried Alan.

"Yes," said the old man. "How carefully she will look after you! She will never allow you to be tired, to sit in a *draught, to neglect your food. If you are an hour late, she will be terrified. She will think you are killed, or that some *siren has caught you."

"I can hardly imagine Diana like that!" cried Alan, overwhelmed with joy.

"You will not have to use your imagination," said the old man. "And, by the way, since there are always sirens, if by any chance you *should*, later on, slip a little, you need not worry. She will forgive you, in the end. She will be terribly hurt, of course, but she will forgive you—in the end."

"That will not happen," said Alan *fervently.

"Of course not," said the old man. "But, if it did, you need not worry. She would never divorce you. Oh, no! And, of course, she herself will never give you the least, the very least, *grounds for—uneasiness."

"And how much," said Alan, "is this wonderful mixture?"

"It is not as *dear," said the old man, "as the glove-cleaner, or life-cleaner, as I sometimes call it. No. That is five thousand dollars, never a penny less. One has to be older than you are, to indulge in that sort of thing. One has to save up for it."

"But the love potion?" said Alan.

"Oh, that," said the old man, opening the drawer in the kitchen table, and taking out a tiny, rather dirty-looking *phial. "That is just a dollar."

"I can't tell you how grateful I am," said Alan, watching him fill it.

"I like to oblige," said the old man. "Then customers come back, later in life, when they are *rather better off, and want more expensive things. Here you are. You will find it very effective."

"Thank you again," said Alan. "Good-by."

"*Au revoir," said the old man.

Glossary

apprehensively   worriedly, fearfully

au revoir   Good-by until we meet again (French)

autopsy   the medical examination of a body to determine the cause of death

bountifully   generously, in great quantity

buff-colored   a pale yellowish-brown

chaser   a drink of water or beer taken after a drink of hard liquor (informal)

costly   expensive

dear   expensive

draught   chiefly-British spelling of **draft** "a current of air." *The choice of spelling is consistent with the old man's rather formal style of speech.*

er   *The word Alan is too shy to say is* **aphrodisiac** *"arousing sexual passion."*

fervently   with great sincerity and passion

five thousand dollars   *Given his modest style of life (and New York prices at the time the story was written), this would be enough to support the old man for a year.*

giddy   silly, not serious toward life

grounds   basis, reason

had been told   *by the person who sent him*

imperceptible   not able to be seen

kitten   a baby cat

landing   the area at the top of a flight of stairs

laxative   a medicine or drug that causes a bowel movement

peered about   looked around intently, unable to see well

Pell Street   a rather poor street in New York's Chinatown

phial   a small glass tube

please   satisfy

potion   a (magic) liquid, most often associated with love

rapture   state of great happiness

rather better off   wealthier, richer

rocking-chair   a chair mounted on curved pieces of wood which enable it to rock back and forth

siren   a seductive woman

sole only

teaspoonful five liquid grams

teething mixture a medicine to lessen the pain of a baby's teeth
 growing in

Comprehension and Discussion Questions

*1. What kind of a building does Alan go into? Office or residential? Old or new? Well kept up or shabby?

2. Why does he enter without ringing the bell or knocking?

3. What is there in the room?

4. How does the old man know Alan's name?

*5 What sort of products does the old man have for sale? Do you think he has many customers? Why?

6. What is the "life-cleaner"? How much does it cost?

*7. What does the old man mean when he says "Young people who need a love potion very seldom have five thousand dollars. Otherwise they would not need a love potion"?

*8. What is the old man's sales philosophy?

9. Are the physical effects of the love potion temporary or long-lasting? Slight or great?

*10. How will Diana's attitude toward Alan change after she has drunk the potion?

11. Will Diana ever tire of Alan or become angry with him? Will she ever be unfaithful to him?

*12. Where does the old man keep the love potion? How much does it cost? Why do you think it is so inexpensive?

*13. Why does the old man say *au revoir*?

*14. What does the title of the story imply?

 * *These questions are the most important for class discussion.*

Exercises

A. ANTONYMS. Match each adjective in Column I with the word in Column II which means the opposite.

I	II
Ex. apprehensive (*CALM*)	adoring
1. casual	calm
2. costly	despairing
3. dim	inexpensive
4. imperceptible	interested
5. indifferent	limited
6. polite	long-lasting
7. rapturous	noticeable
8. scornful	rude
9. varied	well-lit

B. WORD CHOICE. Now choose the most appropriate words among those in Columns I and II above to complete the following sentences.

Ex. As Alan climbed the stairs, he felt *APPREHENSIVE*.

1. The name was hard to read because the light was _____.
2. "I am glad to make your acquaintance" is an extremely _____ greeting.
3. The old man's stock was much more _____ than that of a drugstore.
4. The taste of a poison shouldn't be _____ to the victim.
5. Five thousand dollars for a teaspoonful of liquid is certainly _____!
6. Alan tried to pretend that he was _____ to the aphrodisiac effects of the love potion.
7. The effects of the love potion were guaranteed to be _____.
8. Alan was _____ at the idea of having Diana's total devotion for the rest of his life.
9. The old man wasn't the least bit _____ in Alan's enthusiastic belief in the joys of marriage to Diana.

C. STYLISTIC VARIATION. Make the style of these sentences more casual EITHER by replacing the italicized expression OR by using the negative contraction N'T with the verb.

Ex. The room contained *no furniture but* a table.
THE ROOM CONTAINED *ONLY* A TABLE.

"I want *nothing* of that sort."
"*I DON'T WANT ANYTHING* OF THAT SORT."

1. "My stock in trade is *not very large*."

2. "Young people who need a love potion *very seldom* have five thousand dollars."

3. "I hope *all* your mixtures are *not as* expensive."

4. "It would be *no good* charging that sort of price."

5. "You *need not* worry."

D. DRAMATIZATION. In class, read the story as a play, with each member of the class reading one or two speeches (the OLD MAN has 22; ALAN has 21). Begin with "Sit down, Mr. Austen" and omit everything not in quotation marks.

Topics for Discussion or Composition

1. What is there in the text to suggest that Alan is a very shy and naive young man? How old do you think he is?
2. What do you suppose the old man sells besides the "life-cleaner" and love potion? There are "perhaps a dozen" bottles and jars on the shelf. Do you think each one contains something different? What similar products might his customers want?
3. The old man guarantees that the love potion will produce all the effects of idealized romantic love. Do you find the sort of life he describes for Alan and Diana appealing?
4. What do you think will happen to Alan and Diana?

WILLIAM CARLOS WILLIAMS

The Use of Force

They were new patients to me, all I had was the name, *Olson. Please come down as soon as you can, my daughter is very sick.

When I arrived I was met by the mother, a big startled looking woman, very clean and apologetic who merely said, Is this the doctor? and let me in. In the back, she added. You must excuse us, doctor, we have her in the kitchen where it is warm. It is very *damp here sometimes.

The child was fully dressed and sitting on her father's *lap near the kitchen table. He tried to get up, but I motioned for him not to bother, took off my overcoat and started to look things over. I could see that they were all very nervous, *eyeing me up and down distrustfully. As often, in such cases, they weren't telling me more than they had to, *it was up to me to tell them; that's why they were spending three dollars on me.

The child was *fairly eating me up with her cold, steady eyes, and no expression to her face whatever. She did not move and seemed, inwardly, quiet; an unusually attractive little thing, and as strong as a *heifer in appearance. But her face was *flushed, she was breathing rapidly, and I realized that she had a high *fever. She had magnificent blonde hair, in *profusion. One of those picture children often reproduced in advertising leaflets and the *photogravure sections of the Sunday papers.

She's had a fever for three days, began the father and we don't know what it comes from. My wife has given her things, you know, like people do, but *it don't do no good. And there's been a lot of sickness around. So we *tho't you'd better *look her over and tell us what is the matter.

As doctors often do I *took a trial shot at it as a point of departure. Has she had a sore *throat?

Both parents answered me together, No...No, she says her throat don't hurt her.

Does your throat hurt you? added the mother to the child. But the little girl's expression didn't change nor did she move her eyes from my face.

Have you looked?

I tried to, said the mother, but I couldn't see.

As it happens we had been having a number of cases of *diphtheria in the school to which this child went during that month and we were all, quite apparently, thinking of that, though no one had as yet spoken of the thing.

Well, I said, suppose we take a look at the throat first. I smiled in my best professional manner and asking for the child's first name I said, come on, Mathilda, open your mouth and let's take a look at your throat.

Nothing doing.

Aw, come on, I *coaxed, just open your mouth wide and let me take a look. Look, I said opening both hands wide, I haven't anything in my hands. Just open up and let me see.

*Such a nice man, put in the mother. Look how kind he is to you. Come on, do what he tells you to. He won't hurt you.

At that I *ground my teeth in disgust. If only they wouldn't use the word "hurt" I might be able to get somewhere. But I did not allow myself to be hurried or disturbed but speaking quietly and slowly I approached the child again.

As I moved my chair a little nearer suddenly with one cat-like movement both her hands *clawed instinctively for my eyes and she almost reached them too. In fact she knocked my glasses flying and they fell, though unbroken, several feet away from me on the kitchen floor.

Both the mother and father *almost turned themselves inside out in embarrassment and apology. You bad girl, said the mother, taking her and shaking her by one arm. Look what you've done. The nice man...

For heaven's sake, I broke in. Don't call me a nice man to her. I'm here to look at her throat on the chance she might have diphtheria and possibly die of it. But that's nothing to her. Look here, I said to the child, we're going to look at your throat. You're old enough to understand what I'm saying. Will you open it now by yourself or shall we have to open it for you?

Not a move. Even her expression hadn't changed. Her breaths however were coming faster and faster. Then the battle began. I had to do it. I had to have a throat *culture for her own protection. But first I told the parents that it was entirely up to them. I explained the danger but said that I would not insist on a throat examination so long as they would take the responsibility.

If you don't do what the doctor says you'll have to go to the hospital, the mother *admonished her severely.

*Oh yeah? I had to smile to myself. After all, I had already fallen in love with the savage *brat, the parents were contemptible to me. In the *ensuing struggle they grew more and more *abject, crushed, exhausted while she surely rose to magnificent heights of insane fury of effort *bred of her terror of me.

The father tried his best, and he was a big man but the fact that she was his daughter, his shame at her behavior and his *dread of hurting her made him release her just at the critical moment several times when I had almost achieved success, till I wanted to kill him. But his dread also that she might have diphtheria made him tell me to go on, go on though he himself was almost fainting, while the mother moved back and forth behind us raising and lowering her hands in an agony of apprehension.

Put her in front of you on your lap, I ordered, and hold both her wrists.

But as soon as he did the child let out a scream. Don't, you're hurting me. Let go of my hands. Let them go I tell you. Then she *shrieked terrifyingly, hysterically. Stop it! Stop it! You're killing me!

Do you think she can stand it, doctor! said the mother.

You get out, said the husband to his wife. Do you want her to die of diphtheria?

Come on now, hold her, I said.

Then I grasped the child's head with my left hand and tried to get the wooden *tongue depressor between her teeth. She fought, with *clenched teeth, desperately! But now I also had grown furious—at a child. I tried to hold myself down but I couldn't. I know how to expose a throat for inspection. And I did my best. When finally I got the wooden *spatula behind the last teeth and just the point of it into the mouth cavity, she opened up for an instant but before I could see anything she came down again and gripping the wooden blade between her *molars she reduced it to *splinters before I could get it out again.

Aren't you ashamed, the mother yelled at her. Aren't you ashamed to act like that in front of the doctor?

Get me a smooth-handled spoon of some sort, I told the mother.

We're going through with this. The child's mouth was already bleeding. Her tongue was cut and she was screaming in wild hysterical shrieks. Perhaps I should have *desisted and come back in an hour or more. No doubt it would have been better. But I have seen at least two children lying dead in bed of neglect in such cases, and feeling that I must get a diagnosis now or never I went at it again. But the worst of it was that I too had got beyond reason. I could have torn the child apart in my own fury and enjoyed it. It was a pleasure to attack her. My face was burning with it.

The damned little brat must be protected against her own idiocy, one says to one's self at such times. Others must be protected against her. It is social necessity. And all these things are true. But a blind fury, a feeling of adult shame, bred of a longing for muscular release are the *operatives. One goes on to the end.

In a final unreasoning assault I overpowered the child's neck and jaws. I forced the heavy silver spoon back of her teeth and down her throat till she *gagged. And there it was—both *tonsils covered with *membrane. She had fought valiantly to keep me from knowing her secret. She had been hiding that sore throat for three days at least and lying to her parents in order to escape just such an outcome as this.

Now truly she *was* furious. She had been on the defensive before but now she attacked. Tried to get off her father's lap and fly at me while tears of defeat blinded her eyes.

Glossary

abject   deserving contempt because behaving in a cowardly or self-abasing manner

admonished   warned

almost turned themselves inside out   *This use of exaggeration for emphasis is typical of American speech.*

brat   a contemptuous word for " child "

bred   past participle (and past tense) of **breed,** here " be the cause of "

clawed   used (her) fingernails to attack, as an animal uses its claws

clenched   held together tightly

coaxed   asked gently, encouragingly

culture   a sample of (throat) tissue to be tested for infection in a laboratory

damp   slightly wet

desisted   stopped

diphtheria   a serious infectious disease of the throat

dread   great fear

ensuing   following

eyeing (me) up and down   looking at (me) from head to toe

fairly eating (me) up   was looking at (me) very intently; here, **fairly** means " almost " (rural colloquialism)

fever   an above-normal body temperature

flushed   red; here, because of a fever

gagged   choked

ground   past tense of **grind** "rub together with great force "

heifer   a young cow

it don't do no good   *Standard English would be " It hasn't done any good." The father's manner of speaking is typical of people with little formal education.*

it was up to (me)   it was (my) responsibility

lap   the front part of a seated person's legs from the waist to the knees

look her over   give her a medical examination

membrane   soft, thin tissue; here, a sign of disease

molars   the back teeth

Oh yeah   Oh yes?; an expression of skepticism (informal)

Olson   a common family name of Scandinavian origin

operatives   here, the immediate, compelling motives

photogravure section   a special section of the weekend newspaper filled with colored pictures reproduced by the photogravure process, in which a picture is reproduced on a metal plate from a photographic negative; the final printing is done from the plate

profusion   abundance

shrieked   screamed

spatula   a tool with a wide, flat, flexible blade; here, it refers to the tongue depressor

splinter   a small, sharp fragment (of wood, glass or metal)

such a nice (man)   *A formula used by mothers to reassure their children about kind strangers.*

tho't   thought

throat   the passage inside the neck

tongue depressor   a thin, flat piece of wood used by a doctor to hold down a patient's tongue in order to examine his throat

tonsils   the two small oval masses of lymphoid tissue in the back of the throat

took a trial shot   made a first attempt; here, an attempt to diagnose the illness

Comprehension and Discussion Questions

	Fact	*Inference & Interpretation**
1.	Who is the narrator, the "I"?	
2.	Whom did he go to see?	What sort of people were the Olsons? Describe each of them. What time of year was it?
3.	Why was the family in the kitchen when the doctor arrived?	
4.	Why did they not tell the doctor "more than they had to"?	The doctor says, "As often, in such cases." What sort of cases does he mean?
5.	How much did the doctor's visit cost?	

6. What did the daughter look like?

    How old do you think the daughter was?

7. What indicated that she was sick?

8. How long had she had a fever? What had her parents done to treat it?

9. What was the doctor's first question? What was the parents' response?

    Why do you think the mother asked her daughter "Does your throat hurt?" when the question had just been answered?

10. What was the doctor's next question? What was the mother's response?

11. What did all three adults fear?

    Why didn't the Olsons speak openly about their fear?

12. What was the child's name?

13. What did the doctor ask her to do?

14. How did the mother try to help the doctor? What was the doctor's reaction?

    Why was the doctor "disgusted" by the mother's approach to her child?

15. What did Mathilda do when the doctor moved closer to her?

    Why did Mathilda react so violently to the doctor?

16. How did the parents react?

    Why were the parents so embarrassed?

17. Why did the doctor object to being called "a nice man"?

18. What did the doctor tell Mathilda to do? How did she react?

19. Why was it so important for the doctor to see the child's throat?

    Why does the doctor describe the final events of the story as a "battle"?

20. How did the mother attempt to force the child to comply?

21. What was the doctor's reaction to the mother's attempt?
22. Why couldn't the father hold his daughter still?

We are told that the father was "a big man" and that "he was almost fainting." Aren't these descriptions contradictory?

23. Why did he insist that the doctor continue trying?
24. What was the mother doing?
25. What did the doctor finally order the father to do?
26. What was the child's reaction?

Why did Mathilda finally break her silence? Or, why had she not spoken before?
Why did the doctor speak so sharply to Mathilda?

27. What did the husband tell his wife to do?
28. What did the doctor use to force open the child's mouth?
29. What did Mathilda do when he had almost succeeded in seeing her throat?
30. What did the doctor use next to force her mouth open?

Why did Mathilda's mother yell at her? What do you think the mother was feeling?
The doctor suddenly shifts from simple to sophisticated vocabulary and sentence structure. What effect does that have?

31. Why did the doctor not wait an hour or two and then try again?
32. What did the doctor find when he finally saw Mathilda's throat?

The doctor says, "I too had got beyond reason." Who else was in that state?
Why had Mathilda lied about having a sore throat?

33. What was Mathilda's reaction when the doctor discovered her "secret"?

Why did she react that way?

* *These questions are the most important for class discussion.*

Exercises

A.   Expressions with LOOK.   Use each of the italicized expressions in an original sentence, illustrating another context in which it could be used.

Ex.   I motioned for him not to bother, took off my overcoat and started to *look things over.*

THE POLICE *LOOKED THINGS OVER* BEFORE THE PARADE.

1.   "We tho't you'd better *look her over.*"

_____

2.   "Let's *take a look* at your throat."

_____

3.   "*Look what* you've *done.*"

_____

4.   "*Look here,*" I said to the child, "we're going to *look at* your throat."

_____

_____

B.   ANTONYMS.   Replace the italicized words with a word or phrase that will reverse the meaning of the sentence.

Ex.   The mother was very *apologetic.*

SELF-CONFIDENT

1.   They were *eyeing* me *up and down.*

_____

2.   *It was up to me* to tell them.

_____

3.   That's *nothing* to her.

_____

4.   In the struggle they grew more *abject, crushed* and *exhausted.*

_____

5.   In a final *unreasoning* assault, I overpowered the child's neck and jaws.

_____

Topics for Discussion or Writing

1. In what way is the parents' reaction to the doctor ambiguous?
2. How much of her parents' attitude toward the doctor does the child accept? In what way(s) does she differ from them?
3. Try to explain these seemingly-contradictory comments of the doctor:
    a. "I had already fallen in love with the savage brat, the parents were contemptible to me."
    b. "But the worst of it was that I too had got beyond reason. I could have torn the child apart in my own fury and enjoyed it. It was a pleasure to attack her. My face was burning with it."
    c. "The damned little brat must be protected against her own idiocy, one says to one's self at such times. One must be protected against her. It is social necessity. And all these things are true. But a blind fury, a feeling of adult shame, bred of a longing for muscular release are the operatives. One goes on to the end."
4. Which character in the story do you feel the most sympathy for? Why?
5. Edmund Burke (1729–1797), an Irish-born English statesman and author who was sympathetic to the cause of the American colonies, wrote:

    > The use of force alone is but *temporary*. It may subdue for a moment; but it does not remove the necessity of subduing again: and a nation is not governed, which is perpetually to be conquered.
    >
    > (*Second Speech on Conciliation with America. The Thirteen Resolutions.*)

    Does it seem likely to you that Williams took his title from Burke? What could the connection in ideas be?

ERNEST HEMINGWAY

The Killers
(Part I)

The door of Henry's *lunchroom opened and two men came in. They sat down at the counter.

"*What's yours?" George asked them.

"I don't know," one of the men said. "What do you want to eat, Al?"

"I don't know," said Al. "I don't know what I want to eat."

Outside it was getting dark. The street-light came on outside the window. The two men at the counter read the menu. From the other end of the counter *Nick Adams watched them. He had been talking to George when they came in.

"I'll have a roast pork tenderloin with apple sauce and mashed potatoes," the first man said.

"It isn't ready yet."

"*What the hell do you put it on *the card for?"

"That's the dinner," George explained. "You can get that at *six o'clock."

George looked at the clock on the wall behind the counter.

"It's five o'clock."

"The clock says twenty minutes past five," the second man said.

"It's twenty minutes fast."

"Oh, to hell with the clock," the first man said. "What have you got to eat?"

"I can give you any kind of sandwiches," George said. "You can have ham and eggs, bacon and eggs, liver and bacon, or a steak."

"Give me *chicken croquettes with green peas and cream sauce and mashed potatoes."

"That's the dinner."

"Everything we want's the dinner, eh? That's the way you work it."

"I can give you ham and eggs, bacon and eggs, liver—"

"I'll take ham and eggs," the man called Al said. He wore a

18

*derby hat and a black overcoat buttoned across the chest. His face was small and white and he had tight lips. He wore a silk *muffler and gloves.

"Give me bacon and eggs," said the other man. He was about the same size as Al. Their faces were different, but they were dressed like twins. Both wore overcoats too tight for them. They sat leaning forward, their *elbows on the counter.

"Got anything to drink?" Al asked.

"*Silver beer, bevo, ginger-ale," George said.

"I mean you got anything to *drink*?"

"Just those I said."

"This is a hot town," said the other. "What do they call it?"

"Summit."

"Ever hear of it?" Al asked his friend.

"No," said the friend.

"What do you do here nights?" Al asked.

"They eat the dinner," his friend said. "They all come here and eat the big dinner."

"That's right," George said.

"So you think that's right?" Al asked George.

"Sure."

"You're a pretty bright boy, aren't you?"

"Sure," said George.

"Well, you're not," said the other little man. "Is he, Al?"

"He's dumb," said Al. He turned to Nick. "What's your name?"

"Adams."

"Another bright boy," Al said. "*Ain't he a bright boy, Max?"

"The town's full of bright boys," Max said.

George put the two *platters, one of ham and eggs, the other of bacon and eggs, on the counter. He set down two *side-dishes of fried potatoes and closed the *wicket into the kitchen.

"Which is yours?" he asked Al.

"Don't you remember?"

"Ham and eggs."

"Just a bright boy," Max said. He leaned forward and took the ham and eggs. Both men ate with their gloves on. George watched them eat.

"What are *you* looking at?" Max looked at George.

"Nothing."

"The hell you were. You were looking at me."

"Maybe the boy meant it for a joke, Max," Al said. George laughed.

"You don't have to laugh," Max said to him. "You don't have to laugh at all, see?"

"All right," said George.

"So he thinks it's all right." Max turned to Al. "He thinks it's all right. *That's a good one."

"Oh, he's a thinker," Al said. They went on eating.

"What's the bright boy's name down the counter?" Al asked Max.

"Hey, bright boy," Max said to Nick. "You go around on the other side of the counter with your boy friend."

"What's the idea?" Nick asked.

"There isn't any idea."

"You better go around, bright boy," Al said. Nick went around behind the counter.

"What's the idea?" George asked.

"None of your damn business," Al said. "Who's out in the kitchen?"

"The *nigger."

"What do you mean the nigger?"

"The nigger that cooks."

"Tell him to come in."

"What's the idea?"

"Tell him to come in."

"Where do you think you are?"

"We know damn well where we are," the man called Max said. "Do we look silly?"

"You talk silly," Al said to him. "What the hell do you argue with this kid for? Listen," he said to George, "tell the nigger to come out here."

"What are you going to do to him?"

"Nothing. *Use your head, bright boy. What would we do to a nigger?"

George opened the slit that opened back into the kitchen. "Sam," he called. "Come in here a minute."

The door to the kitchen opened and the nigger came in. "What was it?" he asked. The two men at the counter took a look at him.

"All right, nigger. You stand right there," Al said.

Sam, the nigger, standing in his *apron, looked at the two men sitting at the counter. "Yes, sir," he said. Al got down from his stool.

"I'm going back to the kitchen with the nigger and bright boy," he said. "Go on back to the kitchen, nigger. You go with him, bright boy." The little man walked after Nick and Sam, the cook, back into the kitchen. The door shut after them. The man called Max sat at the counter opposite George. He didn't look at George but looked in the mirror that ran along back of the counter. Henry's had been made over from a *saloon into a lunch counter.

"Well, bright boy," Max said, looking into the mirror, "why don't you say something?"

"What's it all about?"

"Hey, Al," Max called, "bright boy wants to know what it's all about."

"Why don't you tell him?" Al's voice came from the kitchen.

"What do you think it's all about?"

"I don't know."

"What do you think?"

Max looked into the mirror all the time he was talking. "I wouldn't say."

"Hey, Al, bright boy says he wouldn't say what he thinks it's all about."

"I can hear you, all right," Al said from the kitchen. He had propped open the slit that dishes passed through into the kitchen with a *catsup bottle. "Listen, bright boy," he said from the kitchen to George. "Stand a little further along the bar. You move a little to the left, Max." He was like a photographer arranging for a group picture.

"Talk to me, bright boy," Max said. "What do you think's going to happen?"

George did not say anything.

"I'll tell you," Max said. "We're going to kill a Swede. Do you know a big Swede named Ole Andreson?"

"Yes."

"He comes here to eat every night, *don't he?"

"Sometimes he comes here."

"He comes here at six o'clock, don't he?"

"If he comes."

"We know all that, bright boy," Max said. "Talk about something else. Ever go to the movies?"

"Once in a while."

"You ought to go to the movies more. The movies are fine for a bright boy like you."

"What are you going to kill Ole Andreson for? What did he ever do to you?"

"He never had a chance to do anything to us. *He never even seen us."

"And he's only going to see us once," Al said from the kitchen.

"What are you going to kill him for, then?" George asked.

"We're killing him for a friend. Just to oblige a friend, bright boy."

"Shut up," said Al from the kitchen. "You talk too goddam much."

"Well, I got to keep bright boy amused. Don't I, bright boy?"

"You talk too damn much," Al said. "The nigger and my bright boy are amused by themselves. I got them tied up like a couple of girl friends in the *convent."

"I suppose you were in a convent."

"You never know."

"You were in a *kosher convent. That's where you were."

George looked up at the clock.

"If anybody comes in you tell them the cook is *off, and if they keep after it, you tell them you'll go back and cook yourself. *Do you get that, bright boy?"

"All right," George said. "What you going to do with us afterward?"

"That'll depend," Max said. "That's one of those things you never know at the time."

(continued)

Glossary

ain't   nonstandard negative form of **be** (all persons) in the present tense

apron   a loose garment worn over the front to protect clothes when one is cooking

card   the menu; the list of available dishes, with their prices

catsup   variant spelling of **ketchup**, a spicy tomato sauce served with hamburgers, french fried potatoes and some other dishes

chicken croquettes   finely-chopped pieces of chicken bound together by a thick white sauce, rolled in bread-crumbs and then deep-fried

convent   a Roman Catholic institution where women who have dedicated their lives to the church live in seclusion

derby   a round, stiff hat usually associated with rather formal daytime dress

don't he   substandard for "doesn't he"

Do you get that?   Do you understand? (slang)

elbows on the counter   *The rhyme "Mabel, Mabel, sweet and able/ Keep your elbows off the table." is used in many middle-class American households to remind children of good manners.*

He never even seen us   *The omission of "has" (or "have") in the present perfect is common among uneducated people.*

kosher   here, Jewish; there is no such thing as a "kosher convent"

lunchroom   a small, inexpensive eating place with very simple food

muffler   scarf

Nick Adams   *A character in many of Hemingway's early stories, a stand-in for Hemingway himself.*

nigger   an insulting term for "Negro" (slang)

off   off duty, not working

platter   an oval plate

saloon   a bar; *Saloons traditionally have a long, high mirror behind the counter.*

side-dish   a serving of potatoes, other cooked vegetables, or salad that accompany a meat dish but are served in a separate container; Cf. **side order** a side-dish which is not included in the price of the main dish. *These terms are used in quick-service restaurants.*

silver beer, bevo, ginger-ale   all non-alcoholic beverages. *The story takes place during Prohibition (1920–33), when it was illegal to sell alcoholic beverages in the U.S. The law, however, was widely ignored.*

six o'clock   *The usual dinner hour for many American families.*

That's a good one   a cliché meaning "That statement is amusing"; here, used ironically

Use your head   think

What's yours?   What is your order? *This expression is not impolite in this context, but very informal and restricted to use in lunch-rooms and casual bars.*

What the hell   a common profanity used for emphasis

wicket   a small window through which food is passed from the kitchen

Comprehension and Discussion Questions

*1.   Where does the story take place? What time of day is it? What time of year?

*2.   There are four men in Henry's as the story begins. What do you know about the appearance, personality and social/educational background of each? How much of the information comes from direct description? How much from the way the characters talk and act?

3.   Who is the dominant member of the Max-Al pair? Why do you think so?

*4.   What does Max mean when he says "This is a hot town"?

5.   What do the two men have for dinner? Why do they eat with their gloves on?

6.   What do Max and Al do when they have finished eating?

7.   How do Nick and George differ in their reactions to Max and Al?

8.   What clue is there about George's age, at least relative to that of Max and Al?

9.   Who is Sam? How does he react to Max and Al?

*10. Here is a sketch of what Henry's lunchroom might look like. Where are the various characters after Al has gone into the kitchen with Nick and Sam?

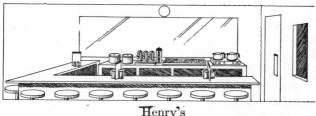

Henry's

*11. What is the story-telling function of the exchanges between Max and George and Max and Al as they wait for Ole to come? Do they, for example, advance the action of the story? Or do they tell you more about one of the characters? Or do they in some way affect your (the reader's) attitude toward the events of the story? Or something else?

*12. What are Max and Al going to do? Why?

13. What does Max tell George to do if any customers come in?

*14. What does Max imply in his answer to George's question "What are you going to do with us afterward"?

* *These questions are the most important for class discussion.*

Exercises

A. THE GOING TO FUTURE. Substitute the word in parentheses in the appropriate place in the preceding sentence, making all other necessary changes. Do the drill orally in class, then write it out.

Ex. They're going to eat dinner.
(have) THEY'RE GOING TO *HAVE* DINNER.
(a sandwich) THEY'RE GOING TO HAVE *A SANDWICH*.

1. (he) _____
2. (a drink) _____
3. (go into the kitchen) _____
_____

4. (they) _____
5. (wait for Ole) _____

_____

6. (see) _____
7. (he) _____
8. (them) _____
9. (be killed) _____

B. *INDIRECT SPEECH.* Change the sentences from direct to indirect speech.

Ex. "What do you want to eat?" he asked them.
HE ASKED THEM *WHAT THEY WANTED TO EAT*.

1. "I don't know," he said.
   He said _____.
2. "I can give you any kind of sandwiches," George said.
   George said _____.
3. "I'll take ham and eggs," Al said.
   Al said _____.
4. "What's your name?" he asked Nick.
   He asked Nick _____.
5. "Which is yours?" he asked Al.
   He asked Al _____.
6. "Hey," Max said to Nick, "you go around to the other side of the counter."
   Max told Nick _____

   _____.
7. "What's the idea?" Nick asked.
   Nick asked _____.
8. "Who's out in the kitchen?" Al asked.
   Al asked _____.
9. "Where do you think you are?" George asked Max and Al.
   George asked Max and Al _____

   _____.
10. "What are you going to do to Sam?" George asked Al.
    George asked Al _____.
11. "All right, stand right where you are," Al said to Sam.
    Al told Sam _____.

C. DRAMATIZATION. In class, act out the first two scenes of the story. Scene 1 has four characters: MAX, AL, NICK and GEORGE. Scene 2 has five characters: the same four plus SAM.

SCENE 1

MAX *and* AL *come into Henry's lunchroom, where* GEORGE, *the counterman, is talking to* NICK ADAMS, *a customer seated at the far end of the counter.* MAX *and* AL *sit down on stools close to the door.*

George: What's yours?

Max: I don't know. What do you want to eat, Al?

Al: I don't know. I don't know what I want to eat.

Max: (reading from the menu) I'll have a roast pork tenderloin with apple sauce and mashed potatoes.

George: It isn't ready yet.

Max: What the hell do you put it on the card for?

George: That's the dinner. You can get that at six o'clock. It's only five o'clock.

Al: The clock says twenty minutes past five.

George: It's twenty minutes fast.

Max: Oh, to hell with the clock. What have you got to eat?

George: I can give you any kind of sandwiches. Or you can have ham and eggs, bacon and eggs, liver and bacon, or a steak.

Max: (still reading from the menu) Give me chicken croquettes with green peas and cream sauce and mashed potatoes.

George: That's the dinner.

Max: Everything we want's the dinner, eh? That's the way you work it.

George: I can give you ham and eggs, bacon and eggs, liver—

Al: (interrupting GEORGE) I'll take ham and eggs.

Max: Give me bacon and eggs.

Al: Got anything to drink?

George: Silver beer, bevo, ginger-ale.

Al: I mean you got anything to *drink*?

George: Just those I said.

Max: This is a hot town. What do they call it?

George: Summit.

Al: Ever hear of it?

Max: No.

Al: What do you do here nights?

Max: They eat the dinner. They all come here and eat the big dinner.

George: That's right.

Al: So you think that's right?

George: Sure.

Al: You're a pretty bright boy, aren't you?

George: Sure.

Max: Well, you're not. Is he, Al?

Al: He's dumb. (*turning to* NICK) What's your name?

Nick: Adams.

Al: Another bright boy. Ain't he a bright boy, Max?

Max: The town's full of bright boys.

George: (*Sets down the two platters of food which have come through the wicket from the kitchen, and brings over two side-dishes of fried potatoes. To* AL) Which is yours?

Al: Don't you remember?

George: Ham and eggs.

Max: Just a bright boy. (*He leans forward and takes the ham and eggs—which* AL *had ordered.* AL *takes the other platter.*
GEORGE *watches the* TWO MEN *eat; both have left their gloves on.*)

Max: What are *you* looking at?

George: Nothing.

Max: The hell you were. You were looking at me.

Al: Maybe the boy meant it for a joke, Max.
(GEORGE *laughs, a bit nervously.*)

Max: *You* don't have to laugh. *You* don't have to laugh at all, see?

George: All right.

Max: (*turning to* AL) So he thinks it's all right. He thinks it's all right. That's a good one.

Al: Oh, he's a thinker. (*The* TWO MEN *go on eating.*)

SCENE 2

Al: What's the bright boy's name down the counter?

Max: (*to* NICK) Hey, bright boy. You go around on the other side of the counter with your boy friend.

Nick: What's the idea?

Max: There isn't any idea.

Al: You better go around, bright boy.

(NICK *goes around behind the counter.*)

George: What's the idea?

Al: None of your damn business. Who's out in the kitchen?

George: The nigger.

Al: What do you mean the nigger?

George: The nigger that cooks.

Al: Tell him to come in.

George: What's the idea?

Al: Tell him to come in.

George: Where do you think you are?

Max: We know damn well where we are. Do we look silly?

Al: You talk silly. What the hell do you argue with this kid for? Listen, tell the nigger to come out here.

George: What are you going to do to him?

Al: Nothing. Use your head, bright boy. What would we do to a nigger?

George: (*opening the wicket*) Sam. Come in here a minute.

Sam: What was it?

Al: All right, nigger. You stand right there.

Sam: Yes, sir.

Al: (*getting down from his stool*) I'm going back to the kitchen with the nigger and bright boy. Go on back to the kitchen, nigger. You go with him, bright boy. (AL, SAM *and* NICK *go into the kitchen, where* AL *ties them up back to back in the corner.*)

Max: (*looking into the mirror behind the counter as he talks*) Well, bright boy, why don't you say something?

George: What's it all about?

Max: (*calling to* AL *in the kitchen*): Hey, Al, bright boy wants to know what it's all about.

Al: Why don't you tell him?

Max: What do you think it's all about?

George: I don't know.

Max: What do you think? (MAX *continues to look in the mirror as he is talking.*)

George: I wouldn't say.

Max: Hey, Al, bright boy says he wouldn't say what he thinks it's all about.

Al: I can hear you, all right. (*to* GEORGE) Listen, bright boy.

Stand a little further along the bar. You move a little to the left, Max.

Max: Talk to me, bright boy. What do you think's going to happen?

(GEORGE *doesn't reply*).

I'll tell you. We're going to kill a Swede. Do you know a big Swede named Ole Andreson?

George: Yes.

Max: He comes here to eat every night, don't he?

George: Sometimes he comes here.

Max: He comes here at six o'clock, don't he?

George: If he comes.

Max: We know all that, bright boy. Talk about something else. Ever go to the movies?

George: Once in a while.

Max: You ought to go to the movies more. The movies are fine for a bright boy like you.

George: What are you going to kill Ole Andreson for? What did he ever do to you?

Max: He never had a chance to do anything to us. He never even seen us.

Al: (*calling from the kitchen*) And he's only going to see us once.

George: What are you going to kill him for, then?

Max: We're killing him for a friend. Just to oblige a friend, bright boy.

Al: Shut up. You talk too goddam much.

Max: Well, I got to keep bright boy amused. Don't I, bright boy?

Al: You talk too damn much. The nigger and my bright boy are amused by themselves. I got them tied up like a couple of girl friends in the convent.

Max: I suppose you were in a convent.

Al: You never know.

Max: You were in a kosher convent. That's where you were.

(GEORGE *looks up at the clock.*)

Max: If anybody comes in you tell them the cook is off, and if they keep after it, you tell them you'll go back and cook yourself. Do you get that, bright boy?

George: All right. What are you going to do with us afterward?

Max: That'll depend. That's one of those things you never know at the time.

ERNEST HEMINGWAY

The Killers
(Part II)

George looked up at the clock. It was a quarter past six. The door from the street opened. A *street-car motorman came in.

"Hello, George," he said. "Can I get supper?"

"Sam's gone out," George said. "He'll be back in about half an hour."

"I'd better go up the street," the motorman said. George looked at the clock. It was twenty minutes past six.

"That was nice, bright boy," Max said. "You're a regular little gentleman."

"He knew I'd blow his head off," Al said from the kitchen.

"No," said Max. "It ain't that. Bright boy is nice. He's a nice boy. I like him."

At six-fifty-five George said: "He's not coming."

Two other people had been in the lunch-room. Once George had gone out to the kitchen and made a ham-and-egg sandwich " *to go" that a man wanted to take with him. Inside the kitchen he saw Al, his derby hat tipped back, sitting on a stool beside the wicket with the *muzzle of a *sawed-off shotgun resting on the ledge. Nick and the cook were back to back in the corner, a towel tied in each of their mouths. George had cooked the sandwich, wrapped it up in oiled paper, put it in a bag, brought it in, and the man had paid for it and gone out.

"Bright boy can do everything," Max said. "He can cook and everything. You'd make some girl a nice wife, bright boy."

"Yes?" George said. "Your friend, Ole Andreson, isn't going to come."

"*We'll give him ten minutes," Max said.

Max watched the mirror and the clock. The hands of the clock marked seven o'clock, and then five minutes past seven.

"Come on, Al," said Max. "We better go. He's not coming."

"Better give him five minutes," Al said from the kitchen. In the five minutes a man came in, and George explained that the cook was sick.

31

"Why the hell don't you get another cook?" the man asked. "Aren't you running a lunch-counter?" He went out.

"Come on, Al," Max said.

"What about the two bright boys and the nigger?"

"They're all right."

"You think so?"

"Sure. We're through with it."

"I don't like it," said Al. "It's *sloppy. You talk too much."

"Oh, what the hell," said Max. "We got to keep amused, haven't we?"

"You talk too much, all the same," Al said. He came out from the kitchen. The cut-off barrels of the shotgun made a slight bulge under the waist of his too tight-fitting overcoat. He straightened his coat with his gloved hands.

"So long, bright boy," he said to George. "*You got a lot of luck."

"That's the truth," Max said. "You ought to *play the races, bright boy."

The two of them went out the door. George watched them, through the window, pass under the *arc-light and across the street. In their tight overcoats and derby hats they looked like a vaudeville team. George went back through the swinging door into the kitchen and untied Nick and the cook.

"I don't want any more of that," said Sam, the cook. "I don't want any more of that."

Nick stood up. He had never had a towel in his mouth before. "Say," he said. "What the hell?" He was trying to *swagger it off.

"They were going to kill Ole Andreson," George said. "They were going to shoot him when he came in to eat."

"Ole Andreson?"

"Sure."

The cook felt the corners of his mouth with his thumbs.

"They all gone?" he asked.

"Yeah," said George. "They're gone now."

"I don't like it," said the cook. "I don't like any of it at all."

"Listen," George said to Nick. "You better go see Ole Andreson."

"All right."

"You better not have anything to do with it at all," Sam, the cook, said. "You better stay way out of it."

"Don't go if you don't want to," George said.

"Mixing up in this ain't going to get you anywhere," the cook said. "You stay out of it."

"I'll go see him," Nick said to George. "Where does he live?" The cook turned away.

"Little boys always know what they want to do," he said.

"He lives up at Hirsch's *rooming-house," George said to Nick.

"I'll go up there."

Outside the arc-light shone through the bare branches of a tree. Nick walked up the street beside the *car-tracks and turned at the next arc-light down a side-street. Three houses up the street was Hirsch's rooming-house. Nick walked up the two steps and pushed the bell. A woman came to the door.

"Is Ole Andreson here?"

"Do you want to see him?"

"Yes, if he's in."

Nick followed the woman up a flight of stairs and back to the end of a corridor. She knocked on the door.

"Who is it?"

"It's somebody to see you, Mr. Andreson," the woman said.

"It's Nick Adams."

"Come in."

Nick opened the door and went into the room. Ole Andreson was lying on the bed with all his clothes on. He had been a *heavyweight prizefighter and he was too long for the bed. He lay with his head on two pillows. He did not look at Nick.

"What was it?" he asked.

"I was up at Henry's," Nick said, "and two fellows came in and tied up me and the cook, and they said they were going to kill you."

It sounded silly when he said it. Ole Andreson said nothing.

"They put us out in the kitchen," Nick went on. "They were going to shoot you when you came in to supper."

Ole Andreson looked at the wall and did not say anything.

"George thought I better come and tell you about it."

"There isn't anything I can do about it," Ole Andreson said.

"I'll tell you what they were like."

"I don't want to know what they were like," Ole Andreson said. He looked at the wall. "Thanks for coming to tell me about it."

"That's all right."

Nick looked at the big man lying on the bed.

"Don't you want me to go and see the police?"

"No," Ole Andreson said. "That wouldn't do any good."

"Isn't there something I could do?"

"No. There ain't anything to do."

"Maybe it was just a *bluff."

"No. It ain't just a bluff."

Ole Andreson rolled over toward the wall.

"The only thing is," he said, talking toward the wall, "I just can't make up my mind to go out. I been in here all day."

"Couldn't you get out of town?"

"No," Ole Andreson said. "I'm through with all that running around."

He looked at the wall,

"There ain't anything to do now."

"Couldn't you fix it up some way?"

"No, I *got in wrong." He talked in the same flat voice. "There ain't anything to do. After a while I'll make up my mind to go out."

"I better go back and see George," Nick said.

"So long," said Ole Andreson. He did not look toward Nick. "Thanks for coming around."

Nick went out. As he shut the door he saw Ole Andreson with all his clothes on, lying on the bed looking at the wall.

"He's been in his room all day," the landlady said downstairs. "I guess he don't feel well. I said to him: 'Mr. Andreson, you ought to go out and take a walk on a nice fall day like this,' but he didn't feel like it."

"He doesn't want to go out."

"I'm sorry he don't feel well," the woman said. "He's an awfully nice man. He was in the *ring, you know."

"I know it."

"You'd never know it except from the way his face is," the woman said. They stood talking just inside the street door. "He's *just as gentle."

"Well, *good night, Mrs Hirsch," Nick said.

"I'm not Mrs. Hirsch," the woman said. "She owns the place. I just look after it for her. I'm Mrs. Bell."

"Well, good night, Mrs. Bell," Nick said.

"Good night," the woman said.

Nick walked up the dark street to the corner under the arc-light, and then along the car-tracks to Henry's eating-house. George was inside, back of the counter. "Did you see Ole?"

"Yes," said Nick. "He's in his room and he won't go out."

The cook opened the door from the kitchen when he heard Nick's voice.

"I don't even listen to it," he said and shut the door.

"Did you tell him about it?" George asked.

"Sure. I told him but he knows what it's all about."

"What's he going to do?"

"Nothing."

"They'll kill him."

"I guess they will."

"He must have *got mixed up in something in Chicago."

"I guess so," said Nick.

"It's a hell of a thing."

"It's an awful thing," Nick said.

They did not say anything. George reached down for a towel and wiped the counter.

"I wonder what he did?" Nick said.

"*Double-crossed somebody. That's what they kill them for."

"I'm going to get out of this town," Nick said.

"Yes," said George. "That's a good thing to do."

"I can't stand to think about him waiting in the room and knowing he's going to *get it. It's too damned awful."

"Well," said George, "you better not think about it."

Glossary

arc-light   the street light

bluff   a threat intended to get results without being carried out

car-tracks   the metal rails that a street-car runs on

double-crossed   cheated, betrayed (slang)

get it   be killed (slang)

Good night, Mrs. Hirsch.   *It is considered polite to address someone by name. Nick is well-mannered.*

got in wrong   became involved with bad people

got mixed up in   became involved in something bad

heavyweight prizefighter   a professional boxer

just as gentle   ~*as can be;* very gentle, nice

muzzle   the firing end of a gun

play the races   bet money on horse races

ring   boxing ring

rooming house   a private home where a person may rent a room inexpensively for a period of months or even years

sawed-off shotgun   a weapon popular with American gangsters in the 1920's and 30's; the front end of the gun is cut off for use at short range; the gun fires a number of pellets at one time

sloppy   careless

street-car motorman   the man who drives a street-car or tram

swagger it off   pretend to be completely unaffected by what has happened

to go   to take out food from the place you bought it in order to eat somewhere else (slang)

We'll give him ten minutes.   We'll wait another ten minutes for him to arrive.

Comprehension and Discussion Questions

1.   Who is the first person to come into the lunchroom while Max and Al are waiting? What time does he come?

THE KILLERS (PART II)/37

2. What does George tell the customer? What does the customer do?
3. Who else comes in between six o'clock and six-thirty-five?
4. What is happening in the kitchen during this time?
5. At what time do Max and Al decide to leave?
*6. How many references to the time are there between the beginning of this part of the story and the line "*Come on, Al*," *Max said.*
*7. What does Al think they should do with George, Sam and Nick? Why?
*8. Max doesn't share Al's opinion. What difference between them does that suggest?
*9. What does Max mean when he tells George that he "ought to play the races"?
*10. What is the effect of describing Max and Al as looking "like a vaudeville team"?
11. What does George do after the killers have left?
12. How do George, Sam and Nick differ in their reactions to what has happened? What suggests that Nick is still in his teens, or at most his early twenties?
*13. What does George ask Nick to do? Why do you think he makes the suggestion?
14. How far is Hirsch's rooming house from Henry's lunchroom?
15. How old do you suppose Ole is? What can you infer about his physical appearance?
16. How does Nick feel as he tells Ole why he has come? What is Ole's reaction?
*17. How does Nick offer to help Ole? Why does Ole refuse all of Nick's offers and suggestions?
18. What is the landlady's opinion of Ole? What effect does that have in relation to the plot?
19. Why do Nick, George and Sam think Ole is going to be killed?
*20. What is Nick going to do?

* *These questions are the most important for class discussion.*

Exercises

A. THE PAST PERFECT. Change the sentences from simple past to past perfect.

Ex. Two more people *came* into the lunchroom.
   TWO MORE PᵀOPLE *H ' ‾ COME* INTO THE LUNCH-ROOM.

1. Once George went out to the kitchen.

   _____

2. He made a ham-and-egg sandwich "to go."

   _____

3. He cooked the egg for the sandwich.

   _____

4. He wrapped the sandwich in oiled paper.

   _____

5. He put the sandwich in a bag.

   _____

6. He brought the sandwich to the man.

   _____

7. The man paid for the sandwich and went out.

   _____

   _____ .

B. NEGATIVE RESPONSES. Pretend that you are Ole and reject each of Nick's suggestions. (For sentences 3, 4 and 6 more than one negative form is possible, as is indicated.)

Ex. You can do something about it.
   NO, I <u>*CAN'T*</u> DO <u>*ANYTHING*</u> ABOUT IT.

1. Do you want to know what they were like?

   _____

2. That would do some good.

   _____

3. There's something you can do.

   (nothing)   _____
   (n't anything)   _____
   (not anything)   _____

4. It's just a bluff.
(n't) _____
(not) _____
5. You could get out of town.

_____

6. There's some way you could fix it up.
(no) _____
(n't any) _____
(not any) _____
7. It'll work out all right.

_____

C. *DRAMATIZATION.* In class, act out the last three scenes of the story. Scene 3 has eight characters: the MOTORMAN, GEORGE, MAX, AL, the FIRST MAN, the SECOND MAN, NICK and SAM. Scene 4 has three characters: a WOMAN, NICK and OLE. Scene 5 has three characters: GEORGE, SAM and NICK.

SCENE 3

Motorman: Hello, George. Can I get supper?
George: Sam's gone out. He'll be back in about half an hour.
Motorman: I'd better go up the street.
  (GEORGE *looks at the clock. It's 6:20.*)
Max: That was nice, bright boy. You're a regular little gentleman.
Al: He knew I'd blow his head off.
Max: No, it ain't that. Bright boy is nice. He's a nice boy. I like him.
First Man: (*entering from the street*) Say, could you give me a ham-and-egg sandwich to go? I'm in kind of a hurry?
George: Ham-and-egg to go. Coming right up. You want that on white?
First Man: Make it whole wheat.
George: Right. Won't be a minute. Cook's just stepped out. (*He goes out to the kitchen to fix the sandwich. When it's ready, he wraps it in waxed paper, puts it in a bag, and brings it out.*) Here you are. That'll be fifteen cents.
First Man: Right. (*He pays for the sandwich.*) Thanks a lot. (*He goes out.*)

Max: Bright boy can do everything. He can cook and everything. You'd make some girl a nice wife, bright boy.

George: Yes? Your friend, Ole Andreson, isn't going to come.

Max: We'll give him ten minutes. (*He watches the clock. The hands show 7:00, then 7:05.*)

Come on, Al. We better go. He's not coming.

Al: Better give him five minutes.

(*A* SECOND MAN *enters from the street.*)

Second Man: What's on the menu for dinner tonight?

George: Gee, I'm sorry. All I can give you is a sandwich. The cook's sick.

Second Man: Why the hell don't you get another cook? (*as he leaves*) Aren't you running a lunch counter?

George: Sorry, mister.

Max: Come on, Al.

Al: What about the two bright boys and the nigger?

Max: They're all right.

Al: You think so?

Max: Sure. We're through with it.

Al: I don't like it. It's sloppy. You talk too much.

Max: Oh, what the hell. We got to keep them amused, haven't we?

Al: You talk too much, all the same. (*He comes out of the kitchen, the shotgun making a slight bulge under his coat. He straightens his coat with his gloved hands. To* GEORGE) So long, bright boy. You got a lot of luck.

Max: That's the truth. You ought to play the races, bright boy. (AL *and* MAX *go out the door.* GEORGE *watches them, then goes back to the kitchen and unties* SAM *and* NICK.)

Sam: I don't want any more of that. I don't want any more of that.

Nick: (*standing up*) Say. What the hell?

George: They were going to kill Ole Andreson. They were going to shoot him when he came in to eat.

Nick: Ole Andreson?

George: Sure.

Sam: (*feeling the corners of his mouth with his thumbs*) They all gone?

George: Yeah. They're gone now.

Sam: I don't like it. I don't like any of it at all.

George: (*to* NICK) Listen. You better go see Ole Andreson.

Nick: All right.

Sam: You better not have anything to do with it at all. You better stay way out of it.

George: Don't go if you don't want to.

Sam: Mixing up in this ain't going to get you anywhere. You stay out of it.

Nick: I'll go see him. Where does he live?

Sam: (*turning away*) Little boys always know what they want to do.

George: He lives up at Hirsch's rooming-house.

Nick: I'll go up there.

SCENE 4

(NICK *goes out of the lunchroom, up the street one block and down a side-street to the third house. He walks up two steps and pushes the bell.*)

Woman: (*opening the door*) Yes?

Nick: Is Ole Andreson here?

Woman: Do you want to see him?

Nick: Yes, if he's in.

Woman: Just follow me. His room is upstairs in the back. (NICK *follows the* WOMAN *up the stairs and back to the end of a corridor. She knocks on the door.*)

Ole: Who is it?

Woman: It's somebody to see you, Mr. Andreson.

Nick: It's Nick Adams.

Ole: Come in. (OLE *is lying on the bed with all his clothes on. He doesn't look at* NICK *as they talk.*)

Ole: What was it?

Nick: I was up at Henry's, and two fellows came in and tied up me and the cook, and they said they were going to kill you. They put us out in the kitchen. They were going to shoot you when you came in to supper. George thought I better come and tell you about it.

Ole: There isn't anything I can do about it.

Nick: I'll tell you what they were like.

Ole: I don't want to know what they were like. Thanks for coming to tell me about it.

Nick: That's all right. (NICK *looks at him.*)
Don't you want me to go and see the police?

Ole: No. That wouldn't do any good.

Nick: Isn't there something I could do?

Ole: No. There ain't anything to do.

Nick: Maybe it was just a bluff.

Ole: No. It ain't just a bluff. (*He rolls over toward the wall.*) The only thing is, I just can't make up my mind to go out. I been in here all day.

Nick: Couldn't you get out of town?

Ole: No. I'm through with all that running around. There ain't anything to do now.

Nick: Couldn't you fix it up some way?

Ole: No, I got in wrong. There ain't anything to do. After a while I'll make up my mind to go out.

Nick: I better go back and see George.

Ole: So long. Thanks for coming around.
(NICK *goes out, closing the door behind him. He goes downstairs.*)

Woman: He's been in his room all day. I guess he don't feel well. I said to him: "Mr. Andreson, you ought to go out and take a walk on a nice fall day like this," but he didn't feel like it.

Nick: He doesn't want to go out.

Woman: I'm sorry he don't feel well. He's an awfully nice man. He was in the ring, you know.

Nick: I know it.

Woman: You'd never know it except from the way his face is. He's just as gentle.

Nick: (*opening the street door to leave*) Well, good night, Mrs. Hirsch.

Woman: I'm not Mrs. Hirsch. She owns the place. I just look after it for her. I'm Mrs. Bell.

Nick: Well, good night, Mrs. Bell.

Woman: Good night.
(NICK *walks back to the lunchroom.*)

SCENE 5

George: Did you see Ole?

Sam: (*opening the door from the kitchen and looking in*) I don't even listen to it. (*He shuts the door again.*)

George: Did you tell him about it?

Nick: Sure. I told him but he knows what it's all about.

George: What's he going to do?

Nick: Nothing.

George: They'll kill him.

Nick: I guess they will.

George: He must have got mixed up in something in Chicago.

Nick: I guess so.

George: It's a hell of a thing.

Nick: It's an awful thing.

(GEORGE *reaches down for a towel and wipes the counter as they both try to think of something more to say.*)

Nick: I wonder what he did?

George: Double-crossed somebody. That's what they kill them for.

Nick: I'm going to get out of this town.

George: Yes. That's a good thing to do.

Nick: I can't stand to think about him waiting in the room and knowing he's going to get it. It's too damned awful.

George: Well, you better not think about it.

Topics for Discussion or Writing

1. Why do Nick, George, Sam and Ole differ as they do in their reactions to the killers? What is *your* feeling about Max and Al? What might they symbolize?
2. How does each of the main characters—Al, Max, Nick, George, Sam, Ole—view the prospect of Ole's death? How do their reactions to his fate differ? How do you think Hemingway wants you, the reader, to feel?
3. What values does Hemingway admire? Do you share his values? For example, do you admire stoicism in the face of death?

JAMES THURBER

The *Unicorn in the Garden

*Once upon a sunny morning a man who sat in a *breakfast nook looked up from his scrambled eggs to see a white unicorn with a gold horn quietly *cropping the roses in the garden. The man went up to the bedroom where his wife was still asleep and woke her. "There's a unicorn in the garden," he said. "Eating roses." She opened one unfriendly eye and looked at him. "The unicorn is a *mythical beast," she said, and turned her back on him. The man walked slowly downstairs and out into the garden. The unicorn was still there; he was now *browsing among the tulips. "Here, unicorn," said the man, and he pulled up a lily and gave it to him. The unicorn ate it *gravely. With a *high heart, because there was a unicorn in his garden, the man went upstairs and *roused his wife again. "The unicorn," he said, "ate a lily." His wife sat up in bed and looked at him, coldly. "You are a *booby," she said, "and I am going to have you put in the *booby-hatch." The man, who had never liked the words "booby" and "booby-hatch," and who liked them even less on a shining morning when there was a unicorn in the garden, thought for a moment. "We'll see about that," he said. He walked over to the door. "He has a golden horn in the middle of his forehead," he told her. Then he went back to the garden to watch the unicorn; but the unicorn had gone away. The man sat down among the roses and went to sleep.

As soon as the husband had gone out of the house, the wife got up and dressed as fast as she could. She was very excited and there was a *gloat in her eye. She telephoned the police and she telephoned a psychiatrist; she told them to hurry to her house and bring a *strait-jacket. When the police and the psychiatrist arrived they sat down in chairs and looked at her, with great interest. "My husband," she said, "saw a unicorn this morning." The police looked at the psychiatrist and the psychiatrist looked at the police. "He told me it ate a lily," she said. The psychiatrist looked at the police and the police looked at the psychiatrist. "He told me it had a golden horn in the middle of its forehead," she said. At a solemn signal from the psychiatrist, the police leaped from their chairs and seized the wife.

44

They had a hard time *subduing her, for she put up a terrific struggle, but they finally subdued her. Just as they got her into the strait-jacket, the husband came back into the house.

"Did you tell your wife you saw a unicorn?" asked the police.

"Of course not," said the husband. "The unicorn is a mythical beast."

"That's all I wanted to know," said the psychiatrist. "Take her away. I'm sorry, sir, but your wife is *as crazy as a jay bird." So they took her away, cursing and screaming, and shut her up in an institution. The husband lived happily ever after.

MORAL: *Don't count your boobies until they are hatched.*

Glossary

as crazy as a jay bird   insane (slang; now out-of-date)

booby   someone who is insane; **booby-hatch** an insane asylum, a hospital for the mentally ill (slang; now out-of-date)

breakfast nook   a corner of the kitchen with a small table and, often, high-backed benches; popular in American homes in the 1930's and 40's

browsing   here, eating slowly, as animals do in a field

cropping   eating; used to describe the way animals eat the top of plants

Don't count your boobies... .   *The actual proverb is* **Don't count your chickens until they are hatched** *meaning "don't count on something before it happens."* Cf. **hatch** to break out of an egg and **hatch** to put someone in a booby-hatch.

gloat   *Thurber invented this noun from the verb* **gloat** *"to look at with selfish delight" and the expression* **to have a gleam in one's eye.**

gravely   seriously

high heart   great happiness

mythical   fictitious, imaginary; adjective form of **myth**

Once upon a   *Children's fairy tales traditionally begin "Once upon a time..." They end with "They all lived happily ever after." This story is from Thurber's FABLES FOR OUR TIME.*

(A **fable** is a short story, often with animals in it, which illustrates a moral. The most famous are those of Aesop and of La Fontaine.)

roused   woke up, awakened

strait-jacket   a white jacket with very long arms, the ends of which are tied behind someone's back to keep him still; used to subdue insane people

subdue   overcome, bring under control

unicorn   an animal like a horse, with a horn in the middle of its forehead

Comprehension and Discussion Questions

Fact	*Inference & Interpretation**
1. What kind of day was it? Where was the man sitting? What was he eating?	What does the setting tell you about the man's style of life?
2. What did he see in the garden? What was it doing?	
3. What did the man do? What was his wife doing?	Why did he want to tell his wife about the unicorn?
4. How did the wife react to her husband's announcement about the unicorn?	What suggests that the husband was disappointed by his wife's reaction?
5. What was the unicorn doing when the man went into the garden?	
6. What did the man do? How did the unicorn react?	Why did it make the man so happy to have a unicorn in his garden?
7. How did the wife respond to the news that the unicorn had eaten a lily?	Was the husband worried by his wife's threat?
8. What did the man do when he found that the unicorn had left?	

9. What did the wife do as soon as her husband had left the house? | Why was there "a gloat" in her eye?

10. Whom did she telephone? What did she tell them? | Why did the police and the psychiatrist look at the woman "with great interest" when they arrived?

11. How did the police and the psychiatrist react to her news about the unicorn? | Why did they have to subdue the wife?

12. When did the husband come back into the house? | Why didn't the husband come as soon as he heard the struggle begin?

13. How did he answer the police's question? | Why did the husband respond as he did to the police's question?

14. Why did the psychiatrist tell the police to take the wife away? | What sort of institution was the wife taken to?

15. What did the husband do? | Explain the moral.

* These questions are the most important for class discussion.

Exercises

A. *Indirect speech with SAY and TELL.* Rewrite these sentences from the story, following the example.

Ex. "There's a unicorn in the garden," he said.

    a) *HE SAID (THAT)* THERE *WAS* A UNICORN IN THE GARDEN.

    b) *HE TOLD HER (THAT)* THERE *WAS* A UNICORN IN THE GARDEN.

1. "The unicorn is a mythical beast," she said.

    a) _____

    b) _____

2. "The unicorn," he said, "ate a lily."
   a) _____
   b) _____
3. "You are a booby," she said, "and I am going to have you put in the booby-hatch."
   a) _____
   b) _____
4. "We'll see about that," he said.
   a) _____
   b) _____
5. "My husband," she said, "saw a unicorn this morning."
   a) _____
   b) _____
6. "He told me it had a golden horn in the middle of its forehead," she said.
   a) _____
   b) _____

B. TRANSFORMING SENTENCES. Each of these sentences can be divided into several shorter sentences, either by eliminating a subordinating word or by adding a few words to a phrase. Rewrite the sentences, underlining words that you add.

Ex. Once upon a sunny morning a man who sat in a breakfast nook looked up from his scrambled eggs to see a white unicorn with a gold horn quietly cropping roses in the garden.
   a) IT WAS A SUNNY MORNING.
   b) A MAN WAS SITTING IN A BREAKFAST NOOK.
   c) HE WAS EATING SCRAMBLED EGGS.
   d) HE LOOKED UP AND SAW A WHITE UNICORN.
   e) THE UNICORN HAD A GOLD HORN.
   f) THE UNICORN WAS QUIETLY CROPPING ROSES IN THE GARDEN.

1. The man went up to the bedroom where his wife was still asleep and woke her.
   a) _____
   b) _____
   c) _____

2. The man, who had never liked the words "booby" and "booby-hatch," and who liked them even less on a shining morning when there was a unicorn in the garden, thought for a moment.

    a) _____
    b) _____
    c) _____
    d) _____

3. As soon as the husband had gone out of the house, the wife got up and dressed as fast as she could.

    a) _____
    b) _____
    c) _____

4. They had a hard time subduing her, for she put up a terrific struggle, but they finally subdued her.

    a) _____
    b) _____
    c) _____

5. So they took her away, cursing and screaming, and shut her up in an institution.

    a) _____
    b) _____
    c) _____

Topics for Discussion or Writing

1. How do the husband and wife differ in temperament and character?

2. In "The Chaser," it is *ironic* that Alan's idealized love may very likely turn to hate. What is the *irony* in this story?

3. "Don't put all your eggs in one basket," is an American proverb similar to the moral of this story. Is there a proverb in your culture which has the same moral?

4. In what ways is Thurber's fable similar to others that you know? In what ways is it different?

JOHN UPDIKE

The *Orphaned Swimming Pool

Marriages, like chemical unions, release upon dissolution packets of the energy locked up in their *bonding. There is the piano no one wants, the *cocker spaniel no one can take care of. Shelves of books suddenly stand revealed as burdensomely dated and unlikely to be reread; indeed, it is difficult to remember who read them in the first place. And what of those old skis in the attic? Or the doll house waiting to be repaired in the basement? The piano goes out of tune, the dog goes *mad. The summer that the Turners got their divorce, their swimming pool had neither a master nor a mistress, though the sun beat down day after day, and a state of *drought was declared in *Connecticut.

It was a young pool, only two years old, of the fragile type fashioned by laying a plastic liner within a carefully carved hole in the ground. The Turners' side yard looked infernal while it was being done; one bulldozer sank into the mud and had to be pulled free by another. But by midsummer the new grass was sprouting, the encircling *flagstones were in place, the blue plastic tinted the water a heavenly blue, and it had to be admitted that the Turners had scored again. They were always a little in advance of their friends. He was a tall, hairy-backed man with long arms, and a nose flattened by *football, and a sullen look of too much blood; she was a fine-boned blonde with dry blue eyes and lips usually held parted and crinkled as if about to ask a worrisome, or *whimsical, question. They never seemed happier, nor their marriage healthier, than those two summers. They grew brown and supple and smooth with swimming. Ted would begin his day with a swim, before dressing to *catch the train, and Linda would hold court all day amid crowds of wet *matrons and children, and Ted would return from work to find a poolside cocktail party in progress, and the couple would end their day at midnight, when their friends had finally left, by swimming nude, before bed. What ecstasy! In darkness the water felt mild as milk and buoyant as helium, and the swimmers became

50

giants, gliding from side to side in a single *languorous stroke.

The next May, the pool was filled as usual, and the usual after-school gangs of mothers and children gathered, but Linda, unlike her, stayed indoors. She could be heard within the house, moving from room to room, but she no longer emerged, as in the other summers, with a cheerful tray of ice and *brace of bottles, and *Triscuits and lemonade for the children. Their friends felt less comfortable about appearing, towels in hand, at the Turners' on weekends. Though Linda had lost some weight and looked elegant, and Ted was cumbersomely jovial, they gave off the faint, sleepless, awkward-making aroma of a couple in trouble. Then, the day after *school was out, Linda *fled with the children to her parents in *Ohio. Ted stayed nights in the city, and the pool was deserted. Though the pump that ran the water through the filter continued to mutter in the *lilacs, the *cerulean pool grew cloudy. The bodies of dead horseflies and wasps dotted the still surface. A speckled plastic ball drifted into a corner beside the diving board and stayed there. The grass between the flagstones grew lank. On the glass-topped poolside table, a spray can of *Off! had lost its pressure and a *gin-and-tonic glass held a *sere mint leaf. The pool looked desolate and haunted, like a stagnant jungle spring; it looked poisonous and ashamed. The postman, stuffing overdue notices and pornography solicitations into the mailbox, averted his eyes from the side yard politely.

Some June weekends, Ted sneaked out from the city. Families driving to church glimpsed him *dolefully sprinkling chemical substances into the pool. He looked pale and thin. He *instructed Roscoe Chace, his neighbor on the left, how to switch on the pump and change the filter, and how much *chlorine and Algitrol should be added weekly. He explained he would not be able to *make it out every weekend—as if the distance that for years he had traveled twice each day, gliding in and out of New York, had become an impossibly steep climb back into the past. Linda, he confided vaguely, had left her parents in *Akron and was visiting her sister in Minneapolis. As the shock of the Turners' joint disappearance wore off, their pool seemed less haunted and forbidding. The Mur-taugh children—the Murtaughs, a rowdy, numerous family, were the Turners' right-hand neighbors—began to use it, without super-vision. So Linda's old friends, with their children, began to *show up, "to keep the Murtaughs from drowning each other." For if anything were to happen to a Murtaugh, the poor Turners (the adjective had become automatic) would be *sued for everything, right when they could least afford it. It became, then, a kind of duty, a test of loyalty, to use the pool.

July was the hottest in twenty-seven years. People brought their own *lawn furniture over in station wagons and set it up. Teenage offspring and Swiss *au-pair girls were established as lifeguards. A nylon rope with flotation corks, meant to divide the wading end from the diving end of the pool, was found coiled in the garage and reinstalled. Agnes Kleefield contributed an old refrigerator, which was wired to an outlet above Ted's basement *workbench and used to store ice, quinine water, and *soft drinks. An *honor system shoebox containing change appeared beside it; a little lost-and-found—an array of forgotten sunglasses, flippers, towels, lotions, paperbacks, shirts, even underwear—materialized on the Turners' side steps. When people, that July, said, "Meet you at the pool," they did not mean the public pool past the shopping center, or the country-club pool beside the *first tee. They meant the Turners'. Restrictions on admission were difficult to enforce tactfully. A visiting Methodist bishop, two Taiwanese economists, an entire girls' softball team from *Darien, an eminent Canadian poet, the archery champion of *Hartford, the six members of a black rock group called the Good Intentions, an ex-mistress of Aly Khan, the *lavender-haired mother-in-law of a Nixon adviser not quite of Cabinet rank, an infant of six weeks, a man who was killed the next day on the *Merritt Parkway, a Filipino who could stay on the pool bottom for eighty seconds, two Texans who kept cigars in their mouths and hats on their heads, three telephone *linemen, four expatriate Czechs, a student Maoist from *Wesleyan, and the postman all swam, as guests, in the Turners' pool, though not all at once. After the daytime crowd *ebbed, and the shoebox was put back in the refrigerator, and the last au-pair girl took the last *goosefleshed, wrinkled child shivering home to supper, there was a tide of evening activity, *trysts (Mrs. Kleefield and the Nicholson boy, most notoriously) and what some called, overdramatically, orgies. True, late splashes and excited *guffaws did often keep Mrs. Chace awake, and the Murtaugh children spent hours at their attic window with binoculars. And there was the evidence of the lost underwear.

One Saturday early in August, the morning arrivals found an unknown car with New York *plates parked in the garage. But cars of all sorts were so common—the parking tangle frequently extended into the road—that nothing much was thought of it, even when someone noticed that the bedroom windows upstairs were open. And nothing came of it, except that around suppertime, in the lull before the evening crowds began to arrive in force, Ted and an unknown woman, of the same physical type as Linda but brunette, swiftly exited from the kitchen door, got into the car, and drove back to New York. The few lingering babysitters and *beaux thus unwittingly glimpsed the root of the divorce. The two lovers had been trapped inside the house all day; Ted was fearful of the *legal consequences of their being seen by anyone who might write and tell Linda. The settlement was at a *ticklish stage; nothing less than terror of Linda's lawyers would have led Ted to suppress his indignation at seeing, from behind the window screen, his private pool turned public carnival. For long thereafter, though in the end he did not marry the woman, he remembered that day when they lived together like fugitives in a cave, feeding on love and ice water, tiptoeing barefoot to the depleted cupboards, which they, arriving late last night, had hoped to stock in the morning, not foreseeing the onslaught of *interlopers that would pin them in. Her hair, he remembered, had tickled his shoulders as she crouched behind him at the window, and through the angry pounding of his own blood he had felt her slim body breathless with the attempt not to giggle.

August drew in, with cloudy days. Children grew bored with swimming. Roscoe Chace went on vacation to Italy; the pump broke down, and no one repaired it. Dead dragonflies accumulated on the surface of the pool. Small deluded toads hopped in and swam around hopelessly. Linda at last returned. From Minneapolis she had gone on to *Idaho for six weeks, to be divorced. She and the children had burnt faces from riding and hiking; her lips looked drier and more quizzical than ever, still seeking to frame that troubling question. She stood at the window, in the house that already seemed to lack its furniture, at the same side window where the lovers had crouched, and gazed at the deserted pool. The grass around it was green from splashing, save where a long-lying towel had smothered a rectangle and left it brown. Aluminum furniture she didn't recognize lay strewn and broken. She counted a dozen bottles beneath the glass-topped table. The nylon divider had parted, and its two halves floated independently. The blue plastic beneath the colorless water tried to make a cheerful, otherworldy statement, but Linda saw that the pool in truth had no bottom, it held bottomless loss, it was one huge blue tear. Thank God no one had drowned in it. Except her. She saw that she could never live here again. In September the place was sold to a family with toddling infants, who for safety's sake have not only drained the pool but have sealed it over with iron pipes and a heavy mesh, and put warning signs around, as around a chained dog.

Glossary

Akron   an industrial city in northern Ohio

au-pair   a girl from overseas who does light housework and/or looks after young children in exchange for room and board (French)

beaux   the plural of **beau** "a young man who is courting a girl" (French); here, it refers to the babysitters' boyfriends

bonding   a **chemical bond** is the force which holds atoms together in a molecule

brace   a pair of two like things; here, two bottles of liquor such as Scotch and gin

catch the train   *Ted was a commuter, taking the train to New York each day to go to the office.*

cerulean   sky blue

chlorine and Algitrol   chemical substances used to keep the pool clean

cocker spaniel   a breed of dog; cockers are popular pets because of their good dispositions and relatively small size

Connecticut   one of the New England states; its southern border is just north of New York City

Darien   a wealthy, fashionable town in Connecticut. *The girls playing softball (a kind of baseball played with a larger, softer ball) were probably in secondary school.*

dolefully   sadly, without enthusiasm

drought   a long period without any rain

ebbed   retreated; describes the action of a receding tide

first tee   the beginning of the golf course

flagstone   a flat, fine-grained stone which is split into slabs and used for paving; it is expensive and is considered quite elegant

fled   past tense of **flee** " to run away, as from danger "

football   *It is not uncommon for an American man to have been injured playing high school or college football.*

gin-and-tonic glass   a tall glass, used for serving a popular summer drink made with gin and quinine water

goosefleshed   skin momentarily covered by small bumps as a result of the cold

guffaw   a loud, sudden laugh

Hartford   the capital of Connecticut; known primarily for the many insurance companies located there

honor system   a system of trust where each person stakes his good name on the fulfillment of his promise; here, to pay for what he ate or drank

Idaho   *Divorce laws vary from state to state, though a divorce granted in one state is valid in all the others; six-weeks' residence qualified Linda to obtain a divorce in this Western state.*

instructed Roscoe Chace   *Suburban neighbors commonly look after each other's homes or yards when one is away.*

interloper   someone who comes without being invited

languorous   sensuously lazy, without effort

lavender-haired   a hair color, a very pale tint of bluish purple. *Some women whose hair has turned white, and who are impressed by their own dignity and elegance as they age, consider it fashionable to have a blue dye added to make the white more brilliant.*

lawn furniture   folding chairs with aluminum frames

legal consequences   *Evidently the divorce was to be on the grounds of incompatibility, rather than adultery, if Linda could prove the latter, she might either refuse Ted the divorce or demand higher alimony payments.*

lilac   a dense bush with sweet-smelling white or purple flowers in spring. *The machinery for cleaning the pool water was concealed in the bushes.*

linemen   men who work outdoors installing or repairing telephone lines

mad   insane

make it out   come out from the city to his home

matron   a married woman
Merritt Parkway   a busy highway in Connecticut
Minneapolis   a city in Minnesota
Off!   a brand of insect-repellent spray
Ohio   a Midwestern state, about 500 miles from Connecticut
orphaned   without parents
plates   license plates
school was out   *American primary and secondary schools are generally in session from early September to early June.*
sere   withered, dry (poetic)
show up   appear, arrive
soft-drinks   non-alcoholic beverages
sued for everything   be required by a court of law to pay a large sum of money in compensation for damages
ticklish   delicate, easily upset
Triscuit   a brand of salty wheat cracker
tryst   a secret, romantic meeting
Wesleyan   a university in western Connecticut
whimsical   fanciful, playful
workbench   a sturdy table. *Many suburban men have a workbench and tools for doing odd jobs.*

Comprehension and Discussion Questions

*1.   To what does Updike compare marriage? What examples does he give to support his contention about marriages that end in divorce?

*2.   What is the implication of the statement "The piano goes out of tune, the dog goes mad"?

3.   What "packet of energy" was released as a result of the dissolution of the Turners' marriage?

4.   How long ago had the Turners' pool been installed? How had it been constructed?

*5.   What is suggested by the phrase "the Turners had scored again"?

6. What did the Turners look like? How old do you think they were? Of what social milieu?

7. What use did they make of the pool during the first two years?

*8. When did signs begin to appear that the Turners' marriage was breaking up? What were the signs?

9. How did the pool's condition deteriorate when the Turners separated?

*10. Where did Ted live after Linda left? Why didn't he stay in the house?

11. Who first began to use the pool again? How did the adults justify using the pool?

12. How soon after the Turners left had the neighbors taken over the pool? How were things organized?

*13. Who swam in the pool besides the Turners' friends? Which of the various "guests" do you think would have been turned away if it could have been done tactfully? Why?

14. What happened at the pool in the evenings? Why did the Murtaugh children spend "hours at their attic window with binoculars"?

15. What did the neighbors do when they noticed a car in the garage and the bedroom windows open? Whom did the car belong to?

16. What was "the root of the divorce"?

*17. How did Ted feel about seeing his private pool being used so freely? Why didn't he say something? Did his companion feel the same way?

18. What happened to the pool in August?

*19. When Linda returned, what was "the troublesome question" her lips seemed to be trying to frame?

*20. What did the pool symbolize for Linda? In what sense had she "drowned" in it?

*21. When the house was sold, what did the new family do with the pool? Why?

*22. What is the effect of the sudden switch from simple past to present perfect tense in the second part of the last sentence of the story?

* *These questions are the most important for class discussion.*

Exercises

A. ARTICLES. Fill the blanks with *a, an, the* or nothing, as required by the context. Be prepared to explain your choices.

It was *A* young pool of _____ fragile type fashioned by laying _____ plastic liner within _____ carefully carved hole in _____ ground. By _____ mid-summer _____ new grass was sprouting, _____ encircling flagstones were in place, _____ blue plastic tinted _____ water _____ heavenly blue, and it had to be admitted that _____ Turners had scored again.

B. PREPOSITIONS. Put each of these prepositions in the appropriate blank: *around, at, for, from, in, in, of, on, on, to, with.*

Children grew bored *WITH* swimming. Roscoe Chace went _____ vacation _____ Italy. Dead dragonflies accumulated _____ the surface _____ the pool. Small deluded toads hopped _____ and swam _____ hopelessly. Linda _____ last returned. _____ Minneapolis she had gone _____ Idaho _____ six weeks, to be divorced.

C. WORD FORMS. For each pair of sentences, change the italicized word in the first sentence to the form (of the same word) which is grammatically appropriate for the second sentence.

Ex. Upon *dissolution*, marriages release packets of energy.
WHEN MARRIAGES *DISSOLVE*, THEY RELEASE PACKETS OF ENERGY.

1. The water felt *buoyant* as helium.
   The water _____ them up.
2. Ted was *cumbersomely* jovial.
   Ted's hearty good humor was _____
3. The bodies of horseflies *dotted* the still surface.
   The bodies of horseflies were like _____ on the still surface.
4. A nylon rope with flotation corks was *reinstalled*.
   The _____ of the nylon rope didn't take long.
5. The goosefleshed, wrinkled children went *shivering* home to dinner.
   The children, goosefleshed and wrinkled, _____ as they went home to dinner.

6. Ted had to suppress his *indignation* at seeing his private pool turned into a public carnival. Ted felt _____ at seeing his private pool turned into a public carnival.

Topics for Discussion or Writing

1. The first paragraph of the story is a statement about divorce. The remaining six paragraphs illustrate the statement by describing an "orphaned" swimming pool. Complete the chart below, then answer the three questions on it.

ANALYSIS BY PARAGRAPH

	Time Covered	Description of Pool
¶1	"THE SUMMER THE TURNERS GOT THEIR DIVORCE"	"THEIR SWIMMING POOL HAD NEITHER MASTER NOR MISTRESS"
¶2		
¶3		
¶4		
¶5		
¶6		
¶7		

a) What time-span does the story cover?

b) In which paragraphs is the pool described as a living thing?

c) In which paragraphs is the pool described as something unpleasant or potentially dangerous?

2. What does the pool symbolize in the story? Why do you think Updike chose to focus on it, rather than on the children, or one of the parents, in discussing the effects of the divorce?

3. Why do you think Ted ran the risk of bringing his mistress to the house when he didn't want any of Linda's friends to know of her existence?

4. What effects of a divorce has Updike chosen not to mention in this story?

SHIRLEY JACKSON

The *Lottery
(Part I)

The morning of June 27th was clear and sunny, with the fresh warmth of a full-summer day; the flowers were blossoming profusely and the grass was richly green. The people of the village began to gather in the square, between the post office and the bank, around ten o'clock; in some towns there were so many people that the lottery took two days and had to be started on June 26th, but in this village, where there were only about three hundred people, the whole lottery took less than two hours, so it could begin at ten o'clock in the morning and still be through in time to allow the villagers to get home for noon dinner.

The children assembled first, of course. School was recently over for the summer, and the feeling of liberty sat uneasily on most of them; they tended to gather together quietly for a while before they broke into *boisterous play, and their talk was still of the classroom and the teacher, of books and *reprimands. Bobby Martin had already stuffed his pockets full of stones, and the other boys soon followed his example, selecting the smoothest and roundest stones; Bobby and Harry Jones and Dicky Delacroix—the villagers pronounced this name "Dellacroy"—eventually made a great pile of stones in one corner of the square and guarded it against the raids of the other boys. The girls stood aside, talking among themselves, looking over their shoulders at the boys, and the very small children rolled in the dust or *clung to the hands of their older brothers or sisters.

Soon the men began to gather, surveying their own children, speaking of planting and rain, tractors and taxes. They stood together, away from the pile of stones in the corner, and their jokes were quiet and they smiled rather than laughed. The women, wearing faded *house dresses, and sweaters, came shortly after their menfolk. They greeted one another and exchanged bits of gossip as they went to join their husbands. Soon the women, standing by their husbands, began to call to their children, and the children came reluctantly, having to be called four or five times. Bobby Martin *ducked under his mother's grasping hand and ran, laughing, back to the pile of stones. His father spoke up sharply, and Bobby came quickly and took his place between his father and his oldest brother.

The lottery was conducted—as were the *square dances, the teen-age club, the *Halloween program—by Mr. Summers, who had time and energy to devote to civic activities. He was a round-faced jovial man and he ran the *coal business, and people were sorry for him, because he had no children and his wife was a *scold. When he arrived in the square, carrying the black wooden box, there was a murmur of conversation among the villagers, and he waved and called, "Little late today, folks." The postmaster, Mr. Graves, followed him, carrying a three-legged stool, and the stool was put in the center of the square and Mr. Summers set the black box down on it. The villagers *kept their distance, leaving a space between themselves and the stool, and when Mr. Summers said, "Some of you fellows want to *give me a hand?" there was a hesitation before two men, Mr. Martin and his oldest son, Baxter, came forward to hold the box steady on the stool while Mr. Summers stirred up the papers inside it.

The original *paraphernalia for the lottery had been lost long ago, and the black box now resting on the stool had been put into use even before Old Man Warner, the oldest man in town, was born. Mr. Summers spoke frequently to the villagers about making a new box, but no one liked to upset even as much tradition as was represented by the black box. There was a story that the present box had been made with some pieces of the box that had preceded it, the one that had been constructed when the first people settled down to make a village here. Every year, after the lottery, Mr. Summers began talking again about a new box, but every year the subject was allowed to fade off without *anything's being done. The black box grew *shabbier each year; by now it was no longer completely black but *splintered badly along one side to show the original wood color, and in some places faded or stained.

Mr. Martin and his oldest son, Baxter, held the black box securely on the stool until Mr. Summers had stirred the papers thoroughly with his hand. Because so much of the ritual had been forgotten or discarded, Mr. Summers had been successful in having slips of paper substituted for the *chips of wood that had been used for generations. Chips of wood, Mr. Summers had argued, had been *all very well when the village was tiny, but now that the population was more than three hundred and likely to keep on growing, it was necessary to use something that would fit more easily into the black box. The night before the lottery, Mr. Summers and Mr. Graves made up the slips of paper and put them in the box, and it was then taken to the safe of Mr. Summers' coal company and locked up until Mr. Summers was ready to take it to the square next morning. The rest of the year, the box was put away, sometimes one place, sometimes another; it had spent one year in Mr. Graves' barn and another year underfoot in the post office, and sometimes it was set on a shelf in the Martin grocery and left there.

There was a great deal of *fussing to be done before Mr. Summers declared the lottery open. There were the lists to make up—of heads of families, heads of *households in each family, members of each household in each family. There was the proper *swearing-in of Mr. Summers by the postmaster, as the official of the lottery; at one time, some people remembered, there had been a recital of some sort, performed by the official of the lottery, a perfunctory, tuneless chant that had been *rattled off *duly each year; some people believed that the official of the lottery used to stand *just so when he said or sang it, others believed that he was supposed to walk among the people, but years and years ago this part of the ritual had been allowed to *lapse. There had been, also, a ritual salute, which the official of the lottery had had to use in addressing each person who came up to draw from the box, but this also had changed with time, until now it was felt necessary only for the official to speak to each person approaching. Mr. Summers was very good at all this; in his clean white shirt and blue jeans, with one hand resting carelessly on the black box, he seemed very proper and important as he talked interminably to Mr. Graves and the Martins.

Just as Mr. Summers finally *left off talking and turned to the assembled villagers, Mrs. Hutchinson came hurriedly along the path to the square, her sweater thrown over her shoulders, and slid into place in the back of the crowd. "*Clean forgot what day it was," she said to Mrs. Delacroix, who stood next to her, and they both laughed softly. "Thought *my old man was *out back stacking wood," Mrs. Hutchinson went on, "and then I looked out the window and the kids was gone and then I remembered it was the twenty-seventh and came *a-running." She dried her hands on her apron, and Mrs Delacroix said, "You're in time, though. They're still talking away up there."

Mrs. Hutchinson *craned her neck to see through the crowd and found her husband and children standing near the front. She tapped Mrs. Delacroix on the arm as a farewell and began to make her way through the crowd. The people separated good-humoredly to let her through; two or three people said, in voices just loud enough to be heard across the crowd, "Here comes *your Missus, Hutchinson," and "Bill, she made it after all." Mrs. Hutchinson reached her husband, and Mr. Summers, who had been waiting, said cheerfully, "Thought we were going to have to *get on without you, Tessie." Mrs. Hutchinson said, grinning, "Wouldn't have me leave *m'dishes in the sink, now, would you, Joe?" and soft laughter ran through the crowd as the people stirred back into position after Mrs. Hutchinson's arrival.

"Well, now," Mr. Summers said soberly, "guess we *better get started, get this over with, *so's we can go back to work. Anybody ain't here?"

"Dunbar," several people said. "Dunbar, Dunbar."

Mr. Summers consulted his list. "Clyde Dunbar," he said. "That's right. He's broke his leg, hasn't he? Who's drawing for him?"

"Me, I guess," a woman said, and Mr. Summers turned to look at her. "Wife draws for her husband," Mr. Summers said. "Don't you have a grown boy to do it for you, Janey?" Although Mr. Summers and everyone else in the village knew the answer perfectly well, it was the business of the official of the lottery to ask such questions formally. Mr. Summers waited with an expression of polite interest while Mrs. Dunbar answered.

"Horace's not but sixteen yet," Mrs. Dunbar said regretfully. "Guess I gotta *fill in for the old man this year."

"Right," Mr. Summers said. He made a note on the list he was holding. Then he asked, "Watson boy drawing this year?"

A tall boy in the crowd raised his hand. "Here," he said. "I'm drawing for m'mother and me." He blinked his eyes nervously and *ducked his head as several voices in the crowd said things like "Good fellow, Jack," and "Glad to see your mother's got a man to do it."

"Well," Mr. Summers said, "guess that's everyone. Old Man Warner make it?"

"Here," a voice said, and Mr. Summers nodded.

(continued)

Glossary

all very well satisfactory; *the phrase is always followed by* **but** *and a contrasting statement, if only by implication*

anything's *the addition of* **'s** *is a rural colloquialism*

a-running *old-fashioned (archaic) verb form;* the **a-** is a verbal prefix meaning " to be in the act of"

better had better, should

boisterous noisy and active

chip small, flat piece

clean completely (rural)

clung past tense of **cling** "hold tightly"; *always followed by* **to** *and a noun*

coal business selling coal to the townspeople for heating their homes

craned stretched

ducked rapidly moved down and to one side; **ducked his head** lowered it in embarrassment

duly in the proper manner and at the proper time; adverbial form of **due**

fill in for substitute for

fussing paying attention to small details

get on begin

give me a hand help me

Halloween October 31, the eve of All Saints' Day (All Hallows' Day). *American children celebrate it by dressing up in costume, carving pumpkins, and playing harmless tricks.*

house dress a simple, inexpensive cotton dress worn for doing housework, rather than for social occasions

households those people living as a separate economic unit

just so in a precise manner

kept their distance were hesitant to approach; stayed away

lapse end without being renewed

left off stopped; past tense of **leave off**

lottery a contest in which tickets are distributed or sold; the winning ticket or tickets are selected in a chance drawing (drawn by lot)

m' my

my old man   my husband (informal)

out back   in the back yard, behind the house

paraphernalia   equipment

rattled off   said mechanically, without thought

reprimand   a reproof, fault-finding, sharp words (from the teacher)

scold   a bad-tempered woman

shabbier   more worn-out, in worse condition

so's   so that (rural)

splintered   with the wood split and coming off in narrow, sharp pieces

square dance   an American folk dance, done with four couples facing each other in a square

swearing-in   the ceremony in which a public official takes his oath of office, formally promising to carry out his duties to the best of his ability

your Missus   your wife (informal)

Comprehension and Discussion Questions

*1.   What time of year is it? Where does the lottery take place? Is this the only lottery being held? Who participates in it?

2.   The lottery is scheduled so as to be over "in time to allow the villagers to get home for noon dinner." Do American families usually eat a large meal together at noon? What does the fact that the families still eat together tell you about the village in the story?

3.   "The children assembled first, of course." Why "of course"?

4.   What do the children do while they are waiting for the lottery to begin?

5.   We are quickly introduced to some of the villagers—Bobby Martin, Bobby and Harry Jones, Dicky Delacroix. How do you know from their names that they are children? Are the family names "Martin" and "Jones" common or unusual in the United States? What about "Delacroix"?

6. How do most of the people in the village earn their living?
*7. In the third paragraph, what suggests that the lottery is a serious event?
8. How are the villagers grouped as the lottery begins?
9. Who conducts the lottery? What other responsibilities does he have in the town?
*10. Who helps Mr. Summers set up the lottery? Why are the villagers reluctant to help?
*11. What paraphernalia is needed for the lottery? How big do you suppose the black box is?
12. What indication do you have of how many years the lottery has been going on?
*13. Who is in favor of making a new black box? Who is opposed? What are the arguments on each side?
*14. What change has Mr. Summers succeeded in making? What argument did he use to convince the people?
15. What do Mr. Summers and Mr. Graves do the night before the lottery?
16. Where is the black box stored when it's not in use?
*17. What activities immediately precede the formal opening of the lottery? How have these activities changed over the years?
18. Why is Mr. Summers thought to be good at conducting the lottery?
19. Who is the last person to arrive? Why is she late?
*20. Why is there "soft laughter" in response to the exchange between Tessie Hutchinson and Joe Summers?
21. Which villager is still missing? Why?
22. What are the rules concerning people who can't attend the lottery?

* *These questions are the most important for class discussion.*

Exercises

A. RURAL SPEECH. The townspeople's speech is typical of that in rural areas, where people sometimes do not have much formal education. Rewrite the sentences, changing the underlined words to conform to standard English.

Ex. "The kids <u>was</u> gone."   THE KIDS <u>WERE</u> GONE.
1. "<u>An body ain't</u> here?"   _____
2. "He's <u>broke</u> his leg, hasn't he?"   _____
3. "Horace's <u>not but</u> sixteen <u>yet</u>."   _____
4. "Guess I <u>gotta</u> fill in for the old man this year."

   _____
5. "Who's drawing for him?" "<u>Me</u>, I guess."   _____

B. TRUNCATED SENTENCES. It is also typical of informal conversation to sometimes omit the subject and/or verb. Add the missing words.

Ex. <u>I'M A</u>   "Little late today, folks."

1. _____ "Some of you fellows want to give me a hand?"
2. _____ "Clean forgot what day it was."
3. _____ "Thought my old man was out back stacking wood."
4. _____ "Wouldn't have me leave m'dishes in the sink now would you, Joe?"
5. _____ "Guess I gotta fill in for the old man this year."
6. _____ "Watson boy drawing this year?"
7. _____ "Glad to see your mother's got a man to do it."
What kinds of subjects and verbs are commonly omitted?

C. WORD FORMS. Change each of the underlined adverbs to a noun, adjective or verb, as required by the modified context.

Ex. The flowers were blossoming <u>profusely</u>.
   THE FLOWERS WERE BLOSSOMING IN <u>PROFUSION</u>.
1. The grass was <u>richly</u> green.
   The grass was a _____ green.
2. School was <u>recently</u> over for the summer.
   The school closing was _____.

3. The feeling of liberty sat <u>uneasily</u> on most of them.
   Most of them felt _____ about their liberty.
4. The children came <u>reluctantly.</u>
   The children were _____ to come.
5. He talked <u>interminably</u> to Mr. Graves and the Martins.
   His conversation with Mr. Graves and the Martins was _____.
6. Mrs. Hutchinson came <u>hurriedly</u> along the path to the square.
   Mrs. Hutchinson _____ along the path to the square.
7. "Well, now," Mr. Summers said <u>soberly,</u> "guess we better get started.
   "Well, now," Mr. Summers said in a _____ tone, "guess we better get started."
8. "Horace's not but sixteen yet," Mrs. Dunbar said <u>regretfully.</u>
   "Horace's not but sixteen yet," Mrs. Dunbar said with _____.

SHIRLEY JACKSON

The Lottery
(Part II)

A sudden hush fell on the crowd as Mr. Summers cleared his throat and looked at the list. "All ready?" he called. "Now, I'll read the names—heads of families first—and the men come up and take a paper out of the box. Keep the paper folded in your hand without looking at it until everyone has had a turn. Everything clear?"

The people had done it so many times that they only half listened to the directions; most of them were quiet, wetting their lips, not looking around. Then Mr. Summers raised one hand high and said, "Adams." A man disengaged himself from the crowd and came forward. "Hi, Steve," Mr. Summers said, and Mr. Adams said, "Hi, Joe." They grinned at one another humorlessly and nervously. Then Mr. Adams reached into the black box and took out a folded paper. He held it firmly by one corner as he turned and went hastily back to his place in the crowd, where he stood a little apart from his family, not looking down at his hand.

"Allen," Mr. Summers said. "Anderson.... Bentham."

"Seems like there's no time at all between lotteries any more," Mrs. Delacroix said to Mrs. Graves in the back row. "Seems like we got through with the last one only last week."

"Time sure goes fast," Mrs. Graves said.

"Clark.... Delacroix."

"There goes my old man," Mrs. Delacroix said. She *held her breath while her husband went forward.

"Dunbar," Mr. Summers said, and Mrs. Dunbar went steadily to the box while one of the woman said, "Go on, Janey," and another said, "There she goes."

"We're next," Mrs. Graves said. She watched while Mr. Graves came around from the side of the box, greeted Mr. Summers gravely, and selected a slip of paper from the box. By now, all through the crowd there were men holding the small folded papers in their large hands, turning them over and over nervously. Mrs. Dunbar and her two sons stood together, Mrs. Dunbar holding the slip of paper.

"Harbut....Hutchinson."

"Get up there, Bill," Mrs. Hutchinson said, and the people near her laughed.

"Jones."

"They do say," Mr. Adams said to Old Man Warner, who stood next to him, "that over in the north village they're talking of *giving up the lottery."

Old Man Warner *snorted. "*Pack of crazy fools," he said. "Listening to the young folks, nothing's good enough for *them*. Next thing you know, they'll be wanting to go back to living in caves, nobody work any more, live *that* way for a while. Used to be a saying about 'Lottery in June, corn be heavy soon.' First thing you know, we'd all be eating *stewed *chickweed and *acorns. There's *always* been a lottery," he added *petulantly. "Bad enough to see young Joe Summers up there joking with everybody."

"Some places have already quit lotteries," Mrs Adams said.

"Nothing but trouble in *that*," Old Man Warner said *stoutly. "Pack of young fools."

"Martin." And Bobby Martin watched his father go forward. "Overdyke....Percy."

"I wish they'd hurry," Mrs. Dunbar said to her older son. "I wish they'd hurry."

"They're almost through," her son said.

"You get ready to run tell Dad," Mrs. Dunbar said.

Mr. Summers called his own name and then stepped forward precisely and selected a slip from the box. Then he called, "Warner."

"Seventy-seventh year I been in the lottery," Old Man Warner said as he went through the crowd. "Seventy-seventh time."

"Watson." The tall boy came awkwardly through the crowd. Someone said, "Don't be nervous, Jack," and Mr. Summers said, "*Take your time, *son."

"Zanini."

After that, there was a long pause, a breathless pause, until Mr. Summers, holding his slip of paper in the air, said, "All right, fellows." For a minute, no one moved, and then all the slips of paper were opened. Suddenly, all the women began to speak at once, saying, "Who is it?" "Who's got it?" "Is it the Dunbars?" "Is it the Watsons?" Then the voices began to say, "It's Hutchinson. It's Bill," "Bill Hutchinson's got it."

"Go tell your father," Mrs. Dunbar said to her older son.

People began to look around to see the Hutchinsons. Bill Hutchinson was standing quiet, staring down at the paper in his hand. Suddenly, Tessie Hutchinson shouted to Mr. Summers, "You didn't give him time enough to take any paper he wanted. I saw you. It wasn't fair!"

"Be a good sport, Tessie," Mrs. Delacroix called, and Mrs. Graves said, "All of us took the same chance."

"Shut up, Tessie," Bill Hutchinson said.

"Well, everyone," Mr. Summers said, "that was done *pretty fast, and now we've got to *be hurrying a little more to get done in time." He consulted his next list. "Bill," he said, "you draw for the Hutchinson family. You got any other households in the Hutchinsons?"

"There's Don and Eva," Mrs. Hutchinson yelled. "Make them take their chance!"

"Daughters draw with their husbands' families, Tessie," Mr. Summers said gently. "You know that as well as anyone else."

"It wasn't fair," Tessie said.

"I guess not, Joe," Bill Hutchinson said regretfully. "My daughter draws with her husband's family, that's only fair. And I've got no other family except the kids."

"Then, as far as drawing for families is concerned, it's you," Mr. Summers said in explanation, "and as far as drawing for households is concerned, that's you, too. Right?"

"Right," Bill Hutchinson said.

"How many kids, Bill?" Mr. Summers asked formally.

"Three," Bill Hutchinson said. "There's Bill, Jr., and Nancy, and little Dave. And Tessie and me."

"All right, then," Mr. Summers said. "Harry, you got *their tickets back?"

Mr. Graves nodded and held up the slips of paper. "Put them in the box, then," Mr. Summers directed. "Take Bill's and put it in."

"I think we ought to start over," Mrs. Hutchinson said, as quietly as she could "I tell you it wasn't *fair*. You didn't give him time enough to choose. *Every*body saw that."

Mr. Graves had selected the five slips and put them in the box, and he dropped all the papers but those onto the ground, where the breeze caught them and lifted them off.

"Listen, everybody," Mrs. Hutchinson was saying to the people around her.

"Ready, Bill?" Mr. Summers asked, and Bill Hutchinson, with one quick glance around at his wife and children, nodded.

"Remember," Mr. Summers said, "take the slips and keep them folded until each person has taken one. Harry, you help little Dave." Mr. Graves took the hand of the little boy, who came willingly with him up to the box. "Take a paper out of the box, Davy," Mr. Summers said. Davy put his hand into the box and laughed. "Take just *one* paper," Mr. Summers said. "Harry, you hold it for him." Mr. Graves took the child's hand and removed the folded paper from the tight fist and held it while little Dave stood next to him and looked up at him wonderingly.

"Nancy next," Mr. Summers said. Nancy was twelve, and her school friends breathed heavily as she went forward, *switching her skirt, and took a slip *daintily from the box. "Bill, Jr.," Mr. Summers said, and Billy, his face red and his feet overlarge, nearly knocked the box over as he got a paper out. "Tessie," Mr. Summers said. She hesitated for a minute, looking around defiantly, and then *set her lips and went up to the box. She snatched a paper out and held it behind her.

"Bill," Mr. Summers said, and Bill Hutchinson reached into the box and felt around, bringing his hand out at last with the slip of paper in it.

The crowd was quiet. A girl whispered, "I hope it's not Nancy," and the sound of the whisper reached the edges of the crowd.

"It's not the way it used to be," Old Man Warner said clearly. "People ain't the way they used to be."

"All right," Mr. Summers said. "Open the papers. Harry, you open little Dave's."

Mr. Graves opened the slip of paper and there was a general sigh through the crowd as he held it up and everyone could see that it was blank. Nancy and Bill, Jr., opened theirs at the same time, and both *beamed and laughed, turning around to the crowd and holding their slips of paper above their heads.

"Tessie," Mr. Summers said. There was a pause, and then Mr.

Summers looked at Bill Hutchinson, and Bill unfolded his paper and showed it. It was blank.

"It's Tessie," Mr. Summers said, and his voice was hushed. "Show us her paper, Bill."

Bill Hutchinson went over to his wife and forced the slip of paper out of her hand. It had a black spot on it, the black spot Mr. Summers had made the night before with the heavy pencil in the coal-company office. Bill Hutchinson held it up, and there was a stir in the crowd.

"All right, folks," Mr. Summers said. "Let's finish quickly."

Although the villagers had forgotten the ritual and lost the original black box, they still remembered to use stones. The pile of stones the boys had made earlier was ready; there were stones on the ground with the blowing scraps of paper that had come out of the box. Mrs. Delacroix selected a stone so large she had to pick it up with both hands and turned to Mrs. Dunbar. "Come on," she said. "Hurry up."

Mrs. Dunbar had small stones in both hands, and she said, gasping for breath, "I can't run at all. You'll have to go ahead and I'll catch up with you."

The children had stones already, and someone gave little Davy Hutchinson a few *pebbles.

Tessie Hutchinson was in the center of a cleared space by now, and she held her hands out desperately as the villagers moved in on her. "It isn't fair," she said. A stone hit her on the side of the head.

Old Man Warner was saying. "Come on, come on, everyone." Steve Adams was in the front of the crowd of villagers, with Mrs. Graves beside him.

"It isn't fair, it isn't right," Mrs. Hutchinson screamed, and then they were upon her.

Glossary

acorn   the fruit of the oak tree, eaten by animals, but not normally by humans

beamed   smiled very happily

be hurrying   hurry; *the use of* **be** *plus the present participle after* **got to** *is now rare except in the phrase* "We've/I've got to be going now."

chickweed   a low, weedy plant, eaten by chickens

daintily   delicately, in a lady-like fashion

giving up   abandoning

held (her) breath   didn't breathe for several seconds

pack   group; *commonly used for* ~ **of cards** *or* ~ **of wolves**

pebble   a tiny stone, such as one finds on a beach

petulantly   with unreasonable irritation

pretty   relatively

set her lips   didn't allow her lips to move, assumed a determined expression

snorted   made a sound of disgust

son   a common way for an older person to address a boy; **sonny** is used with younger boys

stewed   cooked slowly in water for a long period of time

stoutly   with great conviction, with strong belief

switching   casually brushing her skirt with her hand so that it moved as she walked

Take your time   Don't hurry

Comprehension and Discussion Questions

1.   What happens in the first round of drawing? What indication is there in the text that another round is to follow?

*2.   What signs are there of the people's nervousness during the drawing?

3. What clichés about time do Mrs. Delacroix and Mrs. Graves exchange?

*4. Why do the people near Mrs. Hutchinson laugh when she says "Get up there, Bill"? How do you think she feels as she says it? How do the others feel?

5. How does Old Man Warner react to the news that people in another village are talking about giving up the lottery?

*6. What saying about the lottery does Old Man Warner remember? What does that suggest about a possible origin of the lottery?

*7. What arguments does Old Man Warner present for keeping the lottery?

8. How does Mrs. Dunbar show her impatience for the lottery to be over?

9. How many years has Old Man Warner been drawing in the lottery? How old do you suppose he is?

10. Normally someone "wins" a lottery, but that word is never used in the story. What expression is used instead?

*11. A lottery winner is generally very pleased with his luck. How does Bill Hutchinson react when he "gets it"? What is Tessie's reaction? Is her accusation fair?

12. Why do you think her husband speaks sharply to her?

13. Mr. Summers consults "his next list." What was on the first list? What is on the second one?

14. How many "households" are there in the Hutchinson "family"? Who are the members of the household of whicn Bill is the head?

15. For the first round, heads of families—or their representatives —drew. Who draws in the second round, when there is one? Who draws in the final round?

*16. What phrases suggest Mrs. Hutchinson's extreme apprehension—and her efforts to keep it under control?

17. How many papers are in the box for the final drawing? What is done with the other papers?

*18. In what order do the members of the Hutchinson family draw? How do they differ in manner as each goes up to draw?

*19. What prompts Old Man Warner to say "It's not the way it used to be. People ain't the way they used to be"? What do you think he means?

20. In what order are the papers opened? How does the crowd react as each is revealed?
21. Who has drawn the paper with the black spot?
*22. What is the final step of the lottery? Who participates?

* *These questions are the most important for class discussion.*

Exercises

A. *GETOLOGY*.   The verb *get* is used with a variety of meanings in American English, especially in conversation. Replace the underlined phrases with equivalent expressions, eliminating *get* or *got*.

Ex.   "Thought we were going to have to *get on* without you, Tessie."
      BEGIN

1–2.   "Guess we better get started, get this over with."

   _____, _____

3.   "Guess I gotta fill in for the old man this year." _____

4.   "Seems like we got through with the last one only last week."

   _____

5.   "Get up there, Bill." _____

6.   "You get ready to run tell Dad." _____

7.   "Who's got it?" _____

8.   "We've got to be hurrying." _____

9.   "You got any other households in the Hutchinsons?" _____

10.   "And I've got no other family except the kids." _____

11.   "Harry, you got their tickets back?" _____

12.   Billy nearly knocked the box over as he got a paper out.

   _____

B.   SYNONYMS. For each of the underlined words or phrases, provide a word or phrase with a meaning as close as possible to that of the original.

Ex.   A sudden hush fell on the crowd as Mr. Summers cleared his throat and looked at the list.

THE CROWD WAS SUDDENLY QUIET/THE CROWD SUDDENLY GREW QUIET

1. A man disengaged himself from the crowd and came forward.

2. He held it firmly by one corner as he turned and went hastily back to his place in the crowd.

3. "Some places have already quit lotteries," Mrs. Adams said.

4. "Nothing but trouble in that," Old Man Warner said stoutly.

5. "Well, everyone," Mr. Summers said, "that was done pretty fast."

6. He dropped all the papers but those onto the ground where the breeze caught them and lifted them up.

Which do your changes affect more—style or content? And now try your hand at this last sentence.

7. Soft laughter ran through the crowd as the people stirred back into position after Mrs. Hutchinson's arrival.

C.   USED   TO. "Used to be a saying about 'Lottery in June corn be heavy soon.'" "It's not the way it used to be." "People ain't the way they used to be."—Old Man Warner

"Things aren't the way they used to be" is a common complaint among older people. Note that "used to" refers to an *indefinite* time in the past. When the time is specified, *e.g.* "in 1943" or "five years ago," then the simple past tense is used. Also, with "used to" there is an implied contrast with "now."

(1) Write five sentences about changes that have taken place in your hometown since your childhood.

(2) Then write five sentences about changes that have taken place in your country in the last 500 years. Use " used to " in your description.

Ex. (1) THEY *USED TO* SELL ICE CREAM CONES IN THE DRUG STORE, BUT NOW YOU CAN ONLY BUY ICE CREAM IN A PACKAGE.

(2) INDIANS *USED TO* BE THE ONLY INHABITANTS OF NORTH AMERICA, BUT NOW THERE ARE PEOPLE FROM ALL OVER THE WORLD.

Topics for Discussion or Writing

1. Of course such lotteries have never existed. Therefore the story must be an allegory of some sort. For example, it might be a portrayal of fertility rites in primitive cultures or a parody of religious services in modern times. Or is it a commentary on the fragility of family loyalties? What other possibilities occur to you? Which can best be supported by evidence within the text?

2. The lottery is run by two men named "Graves" and "Summers." What significance can you see in the choice of names?

3. Compare and contrast the points of view represented by Mr. Summers and Old Man Warner.

4. Trace the changes in Tessie Hutchinson's attitude in the course of the story. What do these changes suggest about a possible theme for the story?

5. The story is full of details about small-town life, for example, the children's play before the lottery begins. What other details suggest a peaceful rural setting? What is the effect of the contrast between the setting and characters and the plot?

E. B. WHITE

The Hour of Letdown

When the man came in, carrying the machine, most of us looked up from our drinks, because we had never seen anything like it before. The man set the thing down on top of the bar near the *beerpulls. It took up an ungodly amount of room and you could see the bartender didn't like it any too well, having this big, ugly-looking gadget parked right there.

"Two *rye-and-water," the man said.

The bartender went on *puddling an *Old-Fashioned that he was working on, but he was obviously turning over the request in his mind.

"You want a *double?" he asked, after a bit.

"No," said the man. "Two rye-and-water, please." He stared straight at the bartender, not exactly unfriendly but on the other hand not affirmatively friendly.

Many years of *catering to the kind of people that come into saloons had provided the bartender with an adjustable mind. Nevertheless, he did not adjust readily to this fellow, and he did not like the machine—that was sure. He picked up a live cigarette that was *idling on the edge of the cash register, took a *drag out of it, and returned it thoughtfully. Then he poured two shots of rye whiskey, drew two glasses of water, and shoved the drinks in front of the man. People were watching. When something a little out of the ordinary takes place at a bar, the sense of it spreads quickly all along the line and pulls the customers together.

The man gave no sign of being the center of attention. He laid a *five-dollar bill down on the bar. Then he drank one of the ryes and chased it with water. He picked up the other rye, opened a small vent in the machine (it was like an oil cup) and poured the whiskey in, and then poured the water in.

The bartender watched grimly. "Not funny," he said in an even voice. "And furthermore, your companion takes up too much room. "Why'n you put it over on that bench by the door, make more room here."

"There's plenty of room for everyone here," replied the man. "I ain't amused," said the bartender. "Put the goddam thing over near the door like I say. Nobody will touch it."

The man smiled. "You should have seen it this afternoon," he said. "It was magnificent. Today was the third day of the tournament. Imagine it—three days of continuous brainwork! And against the top players in the country, too. Early in the game it gained an advantage; then for two hours it exploited the advantage brilliantly, ending with the opponent's *king backed in a corner. The sudden capture of a knight, the neutralization of a bishop, and it was all over. You know how much money it won, all told, in three days of playing chess?"

"How much?" asked the bartender.

"Five thousand dollars," said the man. "Now it wants to *let down, wants to get a little drunk."

The bartender ran his towel vaguely over some wet spots. "Take it *somewheres else and get it drunk there!" he said firmly. "I got enough troubles."

The man shook his head and smiled. "No, we like it here." He pointed at the empty glasses. "Do this again, will you, please?"

The bartender slowly shook his head. He seemed dazed but *dogged. "You *stow the thing away," he ordered. "I'm not *ladling out whiskey for jokestersmiths."

"'*Jokesmiths,'" said the machine. "The word is 'jokesmiths.'"

A few feet down the bar, a customer who was on his third *highball seemed ready to participate in this conversation to which we had all been listening so attentively. He was a middle-aged man. His necktie was pulled down away from his collar, and he had eased the collar by unbuttoning it. He had *pretty nearly finished his third drink, and the alcohol tended to make him throw his support in with the underprivileged and the thirsty.

"If the machine wants another drink, give it another drink," he said to the bartender. "Let's not have *haggling."

The fellow with the machine turned to his new-found friend and gravely raised his hand to his *temple, giving him a salute of gratitude and fellowship. He addressed his next remark to him, as though deliberately *snubbing the bartender.

"You know how it is when you're all *fagged out mentally, how you want a drink?"

"Certainly do," replied the friend. "Most natural thing in the world."

There was a stir all along the bar, some seeming to side with the bartender, others with the machine group. A tall, gloomy man standing next to me spoke up.

"Another *whiskey sour, Bill," he said. "And *go easy on the lemon juice."

"*Picric acid," said the machine, *sullenly. "They don't use lemon juice in these places."

"That does it!" said the bartender, smacking his hand on the bar. "Will you put that thing away or else *beat it out of here. I ain't in the mood, I tell you. I got this saloon to run and I don't want *lip from a mechanical brain or whatever the hell you've got there."

The man ignored this ultimatum. He addressed his friend, whose glass was now empty.

"It's not just that it's all *tuckered out after three days of chess," he said amiably. "You know another reason it wants a drink?"

"No," said the friend. "Why?"

"It cheated," said the man.

At this remark, the machine chuckled. One of its arms dipped slightly, and a light glowed in a dial.

The friend frowned. He looked as though his dignity had been hurt, as though his trust had been misplaced. "Nobody can cheat at chess," he said. "*Simpossible. In chess, everything is open and above the board. The nature of the game of chess is such that cheating is impossible."

"That's what I used to think, too," said the man. "But there *is* a way."

"Well, it doesn't surprise me any," put in the bartender. "The first time I *laid my eyes on that *crummy thing I spotted it for a crook."

"Two rye-and-water," said the man.

"You can't have the whiskey," said the bartender. He glared at the mechanical brain. "How do I know it ain't drunk already?"

"That's simple. Ask it something," said the man.

The customers shifted and stared into the mirror. We were all in this thing now, up to our necks. We waited. It was the bartender's move.

"Ask it what? Such as?" said the bartender.

"Makes no difference. Pick a couple big figures, ask it to multiply them together. You couldn't multiply big figures together if you were drunk, could you?"

The machine shook slightly, as though making internal preparations.

"Ten thousand eight hundred and sixty-two, multiply it by ninety-nine," said the bartender, viciously. We could tell that he was throwing in the two nines to make it hard.

The machine flickered. One of its tubes spat, and a hand changed position, jerkily.

"One million seventy-five thousand three hundred and thirty-eight," said the machine.

Not a glass was raised all along the bar. People just stared gloomily into the mirror; some of us studied our own faces, others took *carom shots at the man and the machine.

Finally, a youngish, mathematically minded customer got out a piece of paper and a pencil and went into retirement. "It works out," he reported, after some minutes of calculating. "You can't say the machine is drunk!"

Everyone now glared at the bartender. Reluctantly he poured two shots of rye, drew two glasses of water. The man drank his drink. Then he fed the machine its drink. The machine's light grew fainter. One of its cranky little arms wilted.

For a while the saloon simmered along like a ship at sea in calm weather. Every one of us seemed to be trying to digest the situation, with the help of liquor. Quite a few glasses were refilled. Most of us sought help in the mirror—the court of last appeal.

The fellow with the unbuttoned collar *settled his score. He walked stiffly over and stood between the man and the machine. He put one arm around the man, the other arm around the machine. "Let's get out of here and go to a good place," he said.

The machine glowed slightly. It seemed to be a little drunk now.

"All right," said the man. "That suits me fine. I've got my car outside."

He settled for the drinks and put down a tip. Quietly and a

trifle uncertainly he tucked the machine under his arm, and he and his companion of the night walked to the door and out into the street.

The bartender stared fixedly, then resumed his *light house-keeping. "So he's got his car outside," he said, with heavy sarcasm. "Now isn't that nice!"

A customer at the end of the bar near the door left his drink, stepped to the window, parted the curtains, and looked out. He watched for a moment, then returned to his place and addressed the bartender. "It's even nicer than you think," he said. "It's a *Cadillac. And which one of the three of them *d'ya think is doing the driving?"

Glossary

beat it out of here get out, leave immediately (slang)

beerpull the lever to release a flow of beer from a storage tank under the bar

Cadillac one of the most expensive American cars

carom shot in billiards, a shot in which the cue ball hits one ball and then bounces off it to hit another ball

catering to serving the needs of

crummy cheap, shabby (slang)

dogged determined; (pronounced in two syllables; dog-ed)

double two shots (three ounces) of liquor in one glass (slang)

drag an inhalation of cigarette smoke (slang)

d'ya do you

fagged out very tired, completely exhausted (slang)

five-dollar bill *Each drink would have cost around 50¢.*

go easy on don't add too much (informal)

haggling trivial arguing

highball a drink consisting of liquor and water or carbonated beverage served in a tall glass

idling here, burning. *The image is that of a car engine running in neutral gear.*

jokesmith someone who makes jokes; a **smith** is a worker in iron or other metals

king a chess piece, as are **knight** and **bishop**

ladling out literally, serving with a **ladle**, "a long-handled spoon" with a deep bowl

laid (my) eyes on looked at (slang)

let down to let down (its) hair, to relax

light housekeeping doing simple cleaning chores around the house; here, wiping the bar with a towel

lip impertinent, disrespectful talk (slang)

Old-Fashioned a cocktail made of whiskey, bitters, sugar and fruit

picric acid a poisonous, explosive yellow crystalline solid. *The machine is being facetious.*

pretty nearly almost (colloquial)

puddling stirring (slang)

rye whiskey made from rye, a cereal grain

settled his score here, paid his bill
simpossible It's impossible. *The man has had three drinks and his speech is becoming slurred.*
snubbing deliberately ignoring
somewheres *The addition of -s is a colloquialism.*
stow put away
sullenly morosely, sulkily, in an ill-tempered manner
temple the flat part of the head on either side of the forehead
tuckered out tired out, fagged out (slightly more old-fashioned in tone)
whiskey sour a cocktail made with rye whiskey, lemon juice and sugar
Why'n why don't

Comprehension and Discussion Questions

*1. Where is the story set? Who is the narrator?
2. Where did the man put down the machine? Why did that annoy the bartender?
3. What did the man order? Why didn't the bartender serve him immediately?
4. How did the other customers react to the unfolding conflict?
*5. What did the man do with the two drinks? What was the bartender's reaction?
6. How did the man reply when the bartender told him to move the machine?
*7. What had the machine been doing? For how many days? How much money had it won? What reward did it want for its efforts?
8. What was the bartender's reaction to the story of the machine's success?
9. What does the man mean when he says "Do this again"? What words did the bartender use in refusing to serve the man another two drinks?

10. Describe the customer who joined the conversation. How did he begin his participation?

11. How did the man with the machine acknowledge the other customer's support?

*12. Who was in "the machine group" with which some of the customers in the bar sided?

*13. What prompts the bartender to order the man with the machine to either put it away or leave? Why do you think the machine said what it did?

*14. One reason the machine wanted a drink was that it was tired. What was the other reason? What indicates that the machine was proud of what it had done?

*15. How did the friendly customer react to the disclosure of cheating? How did the bartender react?

16. What excuse did the bartender give for refusing to serve the machine a second drink?

17. What test did the man propose to show that his machine wasn't drunk? How did the customers in the bar react?

*18. How long did it take the machine to solve the problem? How long did it take the "youngish, mathematically minded" customer? Was the machine correct?

19. How did the machine react to its second drink?

20. How were the other customers feeling? What did they do to fortify themselves?

*21. What did the friendly customer finally propose? What suggests that he, the man and the machine were all a little drunk?

*22. Did the bartender believe that the man had a car outside? Was it true?

* *These questions are the most important for class discussion.*

Exercises

A. *ARTICLES.* Without looking back at the story, add *a, an, the* or nothing, as required by the context. Be prepared to explain your choices.

"Today was *THE* third day of _____ tournament. Imagine it—_____ three days of _____ continuous brainwork! And against _____ top players in _____ country, too. Early in _____ game it gained _____ advantage; then for _____ two hours it exploited its advantage brilliantly, ending with its opponent's king backed in _____ corner. _____ sudden capture of _____ knight, _____ neutralization of _____ bishop, and it was all over."

B. *ANALYZING SUBORDINATION.* Each of these sentences can be divided into several shorter sentences, either by eliminating a subordinating word or by adding a few words to a phrase. Rewrite the sentences, underlining the words that you add.

Ex. When the man came in carrying the machine, most of us looked up from our drinks, because we had never seen anything like it before.
   a) THE MAN CAME IN.
   b) HE WAS CARRYING A MACHINE.
   c) MOST OF US LOOKED UP FROM OUR DRINKS.
   d) WE HAD NEVER SEEN ANYTHING LIKE IT BEFORE.

1. He picked up a live cigarette that was idling on the edge of the cash register, took a drag out of it, and returned it thoughtfully.
   a) _____
   b) _____
   c) _____
   d) _____

2. When something a little out of the ordinary takes place at a bar, the sense of it spreads quickly all along the line and pulls the customers together.
   a) _____
   b) _____
   c) _____

3. A few feet down the bar, a customer who was on his third highball seemed ready to participate in this conversation to which we had all been listening so attentively.

    a) _____

    b) _____

    c) _____

    d) _____

Topics for Discussion or Writing

1. Only one customer in the bar—a man who was a little high—took an active part in the dispute between the bartender and the man with the machine. Yet everyone was paying attention. Do you think such "non-interference" is typical of big city life? (The story almost certainly takes place in New York City.)

2. The bartender doesn't show any curiosity about the machine. On the contrary, he simply treats it as a disagreeable customer. How do you explain his attitude?

3. What sort of personality does the machine have? What is the man with him like? Would you enjoy meeting them?

4. This story follows the American tradition of the "tall tale"— a seemingly-true story in which some aspects are greatly exaggerated. What aspects of this story couldn't be true?

JESSE STUART

Love

Yesterday when the bright sun blazed down on the *wilted corn my father and I walked around the edge of the new ground to plan a fence. The cows kept coming through the *chestnut oaks on the cliff and running over the young corn. They bit off the tips of the corn and trampled down the *stubble.

My father walked in the *cornbalk. Bob, our *Collie, walked in front of my father. We heard a ground squirrel whistle down over the *bluff among the dead treetops at the clearing's edge. "Whoop, take him, Bob," said my father. He lifted up a young stalk of corn, with wilted dried roots, where the ground squirrel had dug it up for the sweet grain of corn left on its tender roots. This has been a dry spring and the corn has kept well in the earth where the grain has sprouted. The ground squirrels love this corn. They dig up rows of it and eat the sweet grains. The young corn stalks are killed and we have to replant the corn.

I can see my father keep *sicking Bob after the ground squirrel. He jumped over the corn rows. He started to run toward the ground squirrel. I, too, started running toward the clearing's edge where Bob was jumping and barking. The dust flew in tiny swirls behind our feet. There was a cloud of dust behind us.

"It's a big *bull blacksnake," said my father. "Kill him, Bob! Kill him, Bob!"

Bob was jumping and snapping at the snake so as to make it strike and throw itself off guard. Bob had killed twenty-eight *copperheads this spring. He knows how to kill a snake. He doesn't rush to do it. He takes his time and does the job well.

"*Let's don't kill the snake," I said. "A blacksnake is a harmless snake. It kills poison snakes. It kills the copperhead. It catches more mice from the fields than a cat."

I could see the snake didn't want to fight the dog. The snake wanted to get away. Bob wouldn't let it. I wondered why it was crawling toward a heap of black *loamy earth at the *bench of the hill. I wondered why it had come from the chestnut oak sprouts and the matted *greenbriars on the cliff. I looked as the snake lifted its pretty head in response to one of Bob's jumps. "It's not a bull blacksnake," I said. "It's a she-snake. Look at the white on her throat."

"A snake is an enemy to me," my father snapped. "I hate a snake. Kill it, Bob. Go in there and get that snake and quit playing with it!"

Bob obeyed my father. I hated to see him take this snake by the throat. She was so beautifully poised in the sunlight. Bob grabbed the white patch on her throat. He cracked her long body like an ox whip in the wind. He cracked it against the wind only. The blood spurted from her fine-curved throat. Something hit against my legs like pellets. Bob threw the snake down. I looked to see what had struck my legs. It was snake eggs. Bob had slung them from her body. She was going to the sand heap to lay her eggs, where the sun is the *setting-hen that warms them and hatches them.

Bob grabbed her body there on the earth where the red blood was running down on the gray-piled loam. Her body was still *writhing in pain. She acted like a *greenweed held over a new-ground fire. Bob *slung her viciously many times. He cracked her limp body against the wind. She was now limber as a shoestring in the wind. Bob threw her *riddled body back on the sand. She quivered like a leaf in the lazy wind, then her riddled body lay perfectly still. The blood colored the loamy earth around the snake.

"Look at the eggs, won't you?" said my father. We counted thirty-seven eggs. I picked an egg up and held it in my hand. Only a minute ago there was life in it. It was an immature seed. It would not hatch. Mother sun could not *incubate it on the warm earth. The egg I held in my hand was almost the size of a *quail's egg. The shell on it was thin and tough and the egg appeared under the surface to be a watery egg.

"Well, Bob, I guess you see now why this snake couldn't fight," I said, "It is life. Stronger *devour the weaker even among human beings. Dog kills snake. Snake kills birds. Birds kill the butterflies. Man conquers all. Man, too, kills for sport."

Bob was panting. He walked ahead of us back to the house. His tongue was out of his mouth. He was tired. He was hot under his shaggy coat of hair. His tongue nearly touched the dry dirt and white flecks of foam dripped from it. We walked toward the house. Neither my father nor I spoke. I still thought about the dead snake. The sun was going down over the chestnut ridge. A *lark was singing. It was late for a lark to sing. The red evening clouds floated

above the pine trees on our pasture hill. My father stood beside the
path. His black hair was moved by the wind. His face was red in the
blue wind of day. His eyes looked toward the sinking sun.

"And my father hates a snake," I thought.

I thought about the agony women know of giving birth. I thought
about how they will fight to save their children. Then, I thought of
the snake. I thought it was silly for me to think such thoughts.

This morning my father and I *got up with the chickens. He says
one has to get up with the chickens to do a day's work. We got the
*posthole digger, *ax, *spud, measuring pole and the *mattock.
We started for the clearing's edge. Bob didn't go along.

The *dew was on the corn. My father walked behind with the
posthole digger across his shoulder. I walked in front. The wind was
blowing. It was a good morning wind to breathe and a wind that
makes one feel like he can get under the edge of a hill and *heave the
whole hill upside down.

I walked out the corn row where we had come yesterday afternoon. I looked in front of me. I saw something. I saw it move. It
was moving like a huge black rope winds around a *windlass.
"Steady," I *says to my father. "Here is the bull blacksnake."
He took one step up beside me and stood. *His eyes grew wide
apart.

"What do you know about this," he said.

"You have seen the bull blacksnake now," I said. "Take a good
look at him! He is lying beside his dead mate. He has come to her.
He, perhaps, was on her trail yesterday."

The male snake had trailed her to her doom. He had come in the
night, under the roof of stars, as the moon *shed rays of light on
the *quivering clouds of green. He had found his lover dead. He
was coiled beside her, and she was dead.

The bull blacksnake lifted his head and followed us as we walked
around the dead snake. He would have fought us to his death.
He would have fought Bob to his death. "Take a stick," said my
father, "and throw him over the hill so Bob won't find him. Did
you ever see anything to *beat that? I've heard they'd do that.
But this is my first time to see it." I took a stick and threw him
over the bank into the dewy sprouts on the cliff.

Glossary

ax   a tool with a heavy, sharp blade, used for cutting wood

(to) beat that   more astonishing than that (colloquial)

bench   a level, narrow stretch of land (just below the hill)

bluff   a cliff

bull   male

chestnut oak   a tree of eastern and central North America with leaves similar to those of a chestnut tree

Collie   a breed of dog, related to the sheepdog; *"Lassie" is a Collie.*

copperhead   a kind of poisonous snake

cornbalk   the rows of planted corn

devour   eat hungrily or greedily

dew   the moisture on the ground in the morning

got up with the chickens   got up very early

greenbriar   a kind of bush covered with thorns

greenweed   a small shrub with yellow flowers; the weed shrivels and twists when thrown on a fire

heave   move with great effort

His eyes grew wide apart   *A more common phrase is " His eyes grew as big as saucers." Stuart makes effective use of rural metaphors such as this one.*

incubate   to warm (an egg) as by bodily heat, so that the embryo will develop

lark   a bird with a melodious song; larks often live in fields

Let's don't   a rural variant of " Let's not "

loamy   adjective form of **loam** "rich soil "

mattock   a tool used to break up hard ground

posthole digger   a tool for digging holes into which posts are put; a fence will be attached to these posts

quail   a brownish-gray game bird; the eggs are about 1/3 the size of a chicken's eggs

quivering   vibrating

riddled   filled with holes

says   used instead of " said " to give immediacy to a conversational narrative

setting-hen   a hen that sits on eggs to keep them warm until they
 hatch
shed   past tense of **shed** "cast, throw"; *commonly used in the sense
 of* ~ **light on something** *"illuminate"*
sicking   urging (the dog) to attack
slung   past tense of **sling** "throw with force"
spud   a sharp tool used for digging out weeds
stubble   here, the short stalks of corn left after the cows had eaten
 the tender tops
wilted   drooping from heat and lack of water
windlass   a machine for pulling or lifting things by means of a rope
 or chain which is wound around a cylinder or drum and turned
 by a crank
writhing   twisting

Comprehension and Discussion Questions

*1.   Why were the boy and his father walking in the field?
 2.   Why did they need to fence the land?
 3.   Who was with the boy and his father?
 4.   What time of year was it?
 5.   Why did the father want Bob to kill the ground squirrel?
 6.   What did Bob find before he caught the squirrel?
 7.   How did Bob kill a snake? Did he do it skillfully?
*8.   Why did the boy suggest letting the snake live?
 9.   Was the snake willing to fight the dog? Why?
 10.   How did the boy know it was a she-snake rather than a male?
*11.   Why did the father insist that the snake be killed?
*12.   What words suggest that the snake was a beautiful female
 rather than an "enemy"?
*13.   What happened as the dog was killing the snake?
 14.   How many eggs were there? How big were they?
*15.   What pattern does the boy see that he summarizes in his
 statement "It is life"?

16. What time of day was it when they went home?
*17. Why did the snake's death lead the boy to think of child-birth?
*18. Why do you suppose he says "It was silly of me to think such thoughts"?
19. What time did the boy and his father get up the next day? What kind of a day was it?
20. What work did the boy and his father have to do? What did they find when they got to the field?
*21. What can you say about the imagery in the paragraph that begins "The male snake. "?
*22. Why do you think the father told his son to throw the snake over the hill where the dog wouldn't find him?

* *These questions are the most important for class discussion.*

Exercises

A. *IRREGULAR VERBS.* Complete the chart.

	infinitive	simple past	past participle
Ex.	KEEP	kept	KEPT
1.	_____	bit	_____
2.	_____	heard	_____
3.	take	_____	_____
4.	_____	_____	dug
5.	_____	flew	_____
6.	_____	hit	_____
7.	_____	_____	slung
8.	hatch	_____	_____
9.	_____	spoke	_____
10.	_____	grew	_____
11.	_____	_____	seen
12.	_____	shed	_____
13.	_____	_____	fought
14.	_____	threw	_____

B. PREPOSITIONS. Put each of these prepositions in the appropriate blank: *above, against, from, in, of, on, over, through, toward, up.*

Ex. The cows kept coming <u>*THROUGH*</u> the young corn.

1. Bob, our Collie, walked _____ front _____ my father.
2. The squirrels had dug _____ the young corn.
3. The dog jumped _____ the corn rows.
4. I started running _____ the clearing's edge.
5. Something hit _____ my legs like pellets.
6. Bob threw her riddled body back _____ the sand.
7. White flecks of foam dripped _____ his tongue.
8. The red evening clouds floated _____ the pine trees.

C. FIGURATIVE LANGUAGE. Find as many images as you can of birth and death in the story.

birth	*death*
Ex. IT WAS SNAKE *EGGS*.	*DEAD TREETOPS* AT THE CLEARING'S EDGE

Topics for Discussion or Writing

1. What is the effect of setting the story "yesterday" and "this morning" rather than further back in time—or simply using an unspecified past tense?
2. Consider the use of pronouns. What pronoun is used to refer to the dog? When does the pronoun reference to the she-snake shift from "it" to "she"? What pronoun is used to refer to the male snake? What is the effect of these choices?
3. What happens to each of the characters in the story as a result of the events that take place? (*N.b.*, you must first decide who "the characters" are—does that category include the animals, as well as the humans?)
4. What statement about love and hate is the author making? How does hate affect people? How does Stuart's view of love differ from that of Collier in "The Chaser"?
5. What experience have you had—or do you know of—that represents your idea of true love?

JAMES THURBER

The Secret Life of Walter Mitty (Part I)

"We're going through!" The Commander's voice was like thin ice breaking. He wore his full-dress uniform, with the *heavily braided white cap pulled down *rakishly over one cold gray eye. "We can't make it, sir. *It's spoiling for a hurricane, if you ask me." "I'm not asking you, Lieutenant Berg," said the Commander. "Throw on the power lights! *Rev her up to 8,500! We're going through!" The pounding of the cylinders increased: ta-pocketa-pocketa-pocketa-*pocketa-pocketa*. The Commander stared at the ice forming on the pilot window. He walked over and twisted a row of complicated dials. "Switch on No. 8 auxiliary!" he shouted. "Switch on No. 8 auxiliary!" repeated Lieutenant Berg. "Full strength in No. 3 turret!" shouted the Commander. "Full strength in No. 3 turret!" The crew, bending to their various tasks in the huge, *hurtling eight-engined Navy hydroplane, looked at each other and grinned. "The Old Man'll get us through," they said to one another. "The Old Man ain't afraid of Hell!"...

"Not so fast! You're driving too fast!" said Mrs. Mitty. "What are you driving so fast for?"

"Hmm?" said Walter Mitty. He looked at his wife, in the seat beside him, with shocked astonishment. She seemed *grossly unfamiliar, like a strange woman who had yelled at him in a crowd. "You were up to fifty-five," she said. "You know I don't like to go more than forty. You were up to fifty-five." Walter Mitty drove on toward *Waterbury in silence, the roaring of the SN202 through the worst storm in twenty years of Navy flying fading in the remote, intimate airways of his mind. "You're *tensed up again," said Mrs. Mitty. "It's one of your days. I wish you'd let Dr. Renshaw look you over."

Walter Mitty stopped the car in front of the building where his wife went to have her hair done. "Remember to get those *overshoes while I'm having my hair done," she said. "I don't need overshoes," said Mitty. She put her mirror back into her bag. "We've been all through that," she said, getting out of the car. "You're not a young man any longer." He *raced the engine a little. "Why don't you wear your gloves? Have you lost your gloves?" Walter Mitty reached in a pocket and brought out the gloves. He put them on, but after she had turned and gone into the building and he had driven on to a red light, he took them off again. "*Pick it up, brother!" snapped a cop as the light changed, and Mitty hastily pulled on his gloves and *lurched ahead. He drove around the streets aimlessly for a time, and then he drove past the hospital on his way to the parking lot.

... "It's the millionaire banker, Wellington McMillan," said the pretty nurse. "Yes?" said Walter Mitty, removing his gloves slowly. "Who has the case?" "Dr. Renshaw and Dr. Benbow, but there are two specialists here, Dr. Remington from New York and Mr. Pritchard-Mitford from London. He flew over." A door opened down a long, cool corridor and Dr. Renshaw came out. He looked *distraught and *haggard. "Hello, Mitty," he said. "We're *having the devil's own time with McMillan, the millionaire banker and close personal friend of *Roosevelt. *Obstreosis of the ductal tract. *Tertiary. Wish you'd take a look at him." "Glad to," said Mitty.

In the operating room there were whispered introductions: "Dr Remington, Dr. Mitty. Mr. Pritchard-Mitford, Dr. Mitty." "I've read your book on *streptothricosis," said Pritchard-Mitford, shaking hands. "A brilliant performance, sir." "Thank you," said Walter Mitty. "Didn't know you were in the States, Mitty," grumbled Remington. "*Coals to Newcastle, bringing Mitford and me up here for a tertiary." "You are very kind," said Mitty. A huge, complicated machine, connected to the operating table, with many tubes and wires, began at this moment to go pocketa-pocketa-pocketa. "The new anesthetizer is giving way!" shouted an interne. "There is no one in the East who knows how to fix it!" "Quiet, man!" said Mitty, in a low, cool voice. He *sprang to the machine, which was now going pocketa-pocketa-queep-pocketa-queep. He began fingering delicately a row of glistening dials. "Give me a fountain pen!" he snapped. Someone handed him a fountain pen. He pulled a faulty *piston out of the machine and inserted the pen in its place. "That will hold for ten minutes," he said. "Get on with the operation." A nurse hurried over and whispered to Renshaw, and Mitty saw the man turn pale. "*Coreopsis has set in," said Renshaw nervously. "If you would take over, Mitty?" Mitty looked at him and at the *craven figure of Benbow, who drank, and at the grave, uncertain faces of the two great specialists. "If you wish," he said. They slipped a white gown on him; he adjusted a *mask and drew on thin gloves; nurses handed him shining...

"Back it up, *Mac! Look out for that Buick!" Walter Mitty *jammed on the brakes. "Wrong lane, Mac," said the parking-lot attendant, looking at Mitty closely. "Gee. Yeh," muttered Mitty. He began cautiously to back out of the lane marked "Exit Only." "*Leave her sit there," said the attendant. "I'll put her away." Mitty got out of the car. "Hey, better leave the key." "Oh," said Mitty, handing the man the ignition key. The attendant vaulted into the car, backed it up with insolent skill, and put it where it belonged.

They're so damn *cocky, thought Walter Mitty, walking along Main Street; they think they know everything. Once he had tried to take his *chains off, outside *New Milford, and he had got them wound around the *axles. A man had had to come out in a wrecking car and unwind them, a young, grinning garageman. Since then Mrs. Mitty always made him drive to a garage to have the chains taken off. The next time, he thought, I'll wear my right arm in a *sling; they won't grin at me then. I'll have my right arm in a sling and they'll see I couldn't possibly take the chains off myself. He kicked at the *slush on the sidewalk. "Overshoes," he said to himself, and he began looking for a shoe store.

When he came out into the street again, with the overshoes in a box under his arm, Walter Mitty began to wonder what the other thing was his wife had told him to get. She had told him twice, before they set out from their house for Waterbury. In a way he hated these weekly trips to town—he was always getting something wrong. *Kleenex, he thought, *Squibb's, razor blades? No. Toothpaste, toothbrush, *bicarbonate, *carborundum, *initiative and referendum? He gave it up. But she would remember it. "Where's the what's-its-name?" she would ask. "Don't tell me you forgot the what's-its-name." A newsboy went by shouting something about the Waterbury trial.

(continued)

Glossary

axle the rod which passes through the center of a pair of wheels

bicarbonate ~*of soda,* used to calm upset stomachs

carborundum a hard compound of carbon and silicon, used for polishing and grinding

chains used to keep tires from sliding on snow

coals to Newcastle Newcastle, England is a coal-mining center; **to carry coals to Newcastle** means to supply something that is already abundant

cocky conceited, very sure of oneself; like a **cock** "a male chicken"

coreopsis a kind of plant with daisy-like yellow or spotted flowers, from the Latin "resembling a bed bug." *Walter obviously doesn't know the meaning of the word and uses it for its medical sound.*

craven cowardly

distraught preoccupied with troubles

grossly inappropriately, obviously wrong

haggard tired, worn out

having the devil's own time having a lot of difficulty

heavily braided decorated with a lot of white braid, indicating high rank

hurtling moving with great speed and power

initiative and referendum a process by which citizens may propose and vote on legislation

It's spoiling for a hurricane It looks like a hurricane is coming

jammed on the brakes stopped the car suddenly

Kleenex paper handkerchiefs. *The brand name is used here as a generic.*

Leave her sit there. *A better-educated person would say either " Leave it (her) there " or " Let it (her) sit there."*

lurched moved suddenly and jerkily

Mac an all-purpose name for addressing a man whose name you don't know (slang)

mask here, a surgical mask, used to cover a doctor's mouth while he is performing an operation

New Milford a town in Connecticut

obstreosis of the ductal tract   *meaningless terms which, nevertheless, sound impressively medical;* cf., **Obstruction of the digestive tract.** *Walter's imagination leads to a lot of word-play, unintentional on his part.*

overshoes   low rubber boots worn to protect shoes from rain or snow

Pick it up, brother!   Start your car moving again!; **brother** is a very casual form of address (slang)

piston   a tube fitted inside another tube; it moves up and down to give or receive motion

raced the engine   caused the engine to run fast when the gears were disengaged; pushed down on the gas pedal with the car in neutral gear

rakishly   as a nautical term, **rakish** means having a trim, streamlined appearance; here, there is also the connotation of stylish, smart

rev her up   increase the number of revolutions per minute in the engines

Roosevelt   Franklin D., the U.S. president at the time the story takes place

sling   a band of material used to support a broken arm

slush   snow which has built up and begun to melt

sprang   past tense of **spring** "to move quickly and lightly"

Squibb's   short sticks of wood with cotton at each end used for cleaning the ears. *The brand name is used here as a generic.*

streptothricosis   Another invented word; cf. **streptococcus** a kind of bacteria which cause bad sore throats

tensed up   tense, nervous

tertiary   third. *Walter has confused it with* **terminal** *"fatal."*

Waterbury   a city in Connecticut

Comprehension and Discussion Questions

A. *THE FIRST DAYDREAM*
*1. Where is the Commander?
2. How is he dressed?
3. Who is with him?
*4. What problem do they face?
*5. How does the Commander react?

B. *BETWEEN DREAMS*
*1. Where is Walter Mitty? Who is with him?
2. Where are they going?
*3. How fast are they driving? What is the fastest Mrs. Mitty likes to drive?
4. What suggestion does she make about Walter's health?
5. What is Mrs. Mitty going to do?
*6. What is Walter supposed to do while she is busy? Does he want to?
7. What else does she remind him to do?
8. When does Walter take off his gloves? Put them back on?
9. Where is he going to leave the car?
*10. Where does he drive before leaving it?

C. *THE SECOND DAYDREAM*
*1. Match the following descriptions with the characters in Mitty's second daydream.

pretty: _____   Dr. Benbow
rich, influential, seriously ill: _____   Wellington McMillan
nervous, very tired: _____   Dr. Mitty
British medical specialist: _____   Mr. Pritchard-Mitford
American medical specialist:_____   Dr. Remington
modest, always in control: _____   Dr. Renshaw
excitable: _____   the nurse
cowardly, alcoholic: _____   the interne

2 Where does Mitty's second daydream take place?

*3. What previous events are incorporated in the dream?
*4. What does Dr. Remington mean when he says, "Coals to Newcastle, bringing Mitford and me up here for a tertiary"?
5. What is the complicated machine in the operating room?
*6. How does Mitty fix the machine when it starts to break down?
*7. What does the second daydream have in common with the first?

D. *BETWEEN DREAMS*
*1. What brings Walter out of his daydream?
*2. How does the parking lot attendant treat Walter?
*3. How does Walter feel toward the attendant?
*4. What other unfortunate experience had Walter had with the car?
5. When does he plan to have his arm in a sling? Why?
6. What reminds him that he must buy overshoes?
7. What does he do after buying the overshoes?
*8. How often do Walter and his wife go into Waterbury?
*9. What is the connection between the items in the list: "Kleenex, Squibb's, razor blades, toothpaste, toothbrush, bicarbonate, carborundum, initiative and referendum"?

* *These questions are the most important for class discussion.*

Exercises

A. *IRREGULAR VERBS.* Change the form of the italicized verb in the first sentence of each pair to the form appropriate for the second sentence, adding the word(s) in parentheses.
Ex. He *wore* his full-dress uniform.
(probably) TOMORROW HE *WILL PROBABLY WEAR* IT AGAIN.
1. Walter Mitty *drove* on toward Waterbury.
(already) In the past month, he _____
there three times.

2. Renshaw and Benbow *flew* up from New York.
(straight) After they arrived, they learned that Pritchard-Mitford _____ over from London.
3. "Have you *read* Mitty's book on streptothricosis?"
(nearly finished) "I _____ it last night."
4. He *drew* on thin gloves.
(always) His habit was _____ them on carefully.
5. "Be careful not to *wind* the chains around the axles this time," she had said.
(completely) But Walter had got the chains _____ _____ around the axles anyway.

B. SYNONYMS. Replace the italicized words with equivalent expressions.
Ex. He walked over and *twisted* a row of complicated dials.
TURNED
1. He looked at his wife with shocked *astonishment.* _____
2. "I wish you'd let Dr. Renshaw *look you over.*" _____
3. "Didn't know you were in the States, Mitty," *grumbled* Remington. _____
4. He looked at the *grave,* uncertain faces of the two great specialists. _____
5. The attendant *vaulted* into the car. _____

C. DRAMATIZATION. Divide these roles among the members of the class. Scene 1: COMMANDER MITTY, LIEUTENANT BERG, FIRST CREWMAN, SECOND CREWMAN. Scene 2: MRS. MITTY, WALTER, a COP. Scene 3: the pretty NURSE, DR. MITTY, DR. RENSHAW, MR. PRITCHARD-MITFORD, DR. REMINGTON, an INTERNE. Scene 4: the PARKING-LOT ATTENDANT, WALTER, a NEWSBOY.

SCENE 1

Commander Mitty: (*in a voice like thin ice breaking*) We're going through!
Lieutenant Berg: We can't make it, sir. It's spoiling for a hurricane if you ask me

The Commander: I'm not asking you, Lieutenant Berg. Throw on
the power lights! Rev her up to 8,500! We're going through!
(*The pounding of the cylinders increases.* MITTY *stares at
the ice forming on the pilot window. He walks over to the control
panel and twists a row of complicated dials.*)
Switch on No. 8 auxiliary!
Berg: Switch on No. 8 auxiliary!
The Commander: Full strength in No. 3 turret!
Berg: Full strength in No. 3 turret!
First Crewman: The Old Man'll get us through.
Second Crewman: Damn right, he will. The Old Man ain't afraid of
Hell.

SCENE 2

Mrs. Mitty: Not so fast! You're driving too fast! What are you
driving so fast for?
Walter: (*looking at her with shocked astonishment*) Hmm?
Mrs. Mitty: You were up to fifty-five. You know I don't like to
go more than forty. You were up to fifty-five. You're tensed
up again. It's one of your days. I wish you'd let Dr. Renshaw
look you over. (*They pull up to the curb.*) Remember to get
those overshoes while I'm having my hair done.
Walter: I don't need overshoes.
Mrs. Mitty: We've been all through that. You're not a young
man any longer. Why don't you wear your gloves? Have you
lost your gloves? (WALTER *puts on his gloves.*) That's better.
Now don't be late meeting me.
(*Drives away, then stops for a red light. He takes off his gloves.*)
A Cop: Pick it up, brother!
(WALTER *drives on, passing a hospital on his way to the
parking lot.*)

SCENE 3

The Nurse: It's the millionaire banker, Wellington McMillan.
Dr. Mitty: Yes? (*He removes his gloves.*) Who has the case?
The Nurse: Dr. Renshaw and Dr. Benbow, but there are two
specialists here, Dr. Remington from New York and Mr.
Pritchard-Mitford from London. He flew over.
Dr. Renshaw: Hello, Mitty. We're having the devil's own time with

McMillan, the millionaire banker and close personal friend of Roosevelt. Obstreosis of the ductal tract. Tertiary. Wish you'd take a look at him.

Dr. Mitty: Glad to.

(*They go into the operating room.*)

Dr. Renshaw: Dr. Remington, Dr. Mitty. Mr. Pritchard-Mitford, Dr. Mitty.

Mr. Pritchard-Mitford: I've read your book on streptothricosis. A brilliant performance, sir.

Dr. Mitty: Thank you.

Dr. Remington: Didn't know you were in the States, Mitty. Coals to Newcastle, bringing Mitford and me up here for a tertiary.

Dr. Mitty: You are very kind.

Interne: The new anesthetizer is giving way! There is no one in the East who knows how to fix it!

Dr. Mitty: Quiet, man. Give me a fountain pen. (*He inserts it in the place of the faulty piston.*) That will hold for ten minutes. Get on with the operation.

Dr. Renshaw: (*After a whispered consultation with the* NURSE) Coreopsis has set in. If you would take over, Mitty?

Dr. Mitty: If you wish.

SCENE 4

The Parking-Lot Attendant: Back it up, Mac! Look out for that Buick!...Wrong lane, Mac.

Walter: Gee. Yeh.

The Attendant: Leave her sit there. I'll put her away. (*As* WALTER *is getting out*) Hey, better leave the key.

Walter: Oh. (*He hands the key to the* ATTENDANT. *Talking to himself as he walks away*)

They're so damn cocky. They think they know everything. Like the time I accidentally got the chains wrapped around the axles and that young garage man who came out in the wrecking car couldn't stop grinning. Yeah, now they always look so superior in the garage when we go to have the chains taken off.

(*Still talking to himself*) The next time, I'll wear my right arm in a sling. They won't grin at me then. I'll have my right arm in a sling and they'll see I couldn't possibly take the chains off myself. (*He kicks at the slush on the sidewalk.*) Overshoes.

(*He goes into a shoestore. When he comes out, he tries to think of the second thing he was supposed to buy.*) Kleenex, Squibb's, razor blades? No. Toothpaste, toothbrush, bicarbonate, carborundum, initiative and referendum? No, I give up. But she'll remember. She'll ask me "Where's the what's-its-name? Don't tell me you forgot the what's-its-name?"

Newsboy: Read all about it! New developments in Waterbury murder trial! Read all about it!

JAMES THURBER

The Secret Life of Walter Mitty (Part II)

... "Perhaps this will refresh your memory." The *District Attorney suddenly thrust a heavy automatic at the quiet figure on the witness stand. "Have you ever seen this before?" Walter Mitty took the gun and examined it expertly. "This is my *Webley-Vickers 50.80," he said calmly. An excited buzz ran around the courtroom. The judge rapped for order. "You are a *crack shot with any sort of firearms, I believe?" said the District Attorney, *insinuatingly. "Objection!" shouted Mitty's attorney. "We have shown that the defendant could not have fired the shot. We have shown that he wore his right arm in a sling on the night of the fourteenth of July." Walter Mitty raised his hand briefly and the *bickering attorneys were stilled. "With any known make of gun," he said evenly, "I could have killed Gregory Fitzhurst at three hundred feet *with my left hand.* *Pandemonium broke loose in the courtroom. A woman's scream rose above the bedlam and suddenly a lovely, dark-haired girl was in Walter Mitty's arms. The District Attorney struck at her savagely. Without rising from his chair, Mitty *let the man have it on the point of the chin. "You miserable *cur!"...

"*Puppy biscuit," said Walter Mitty. He stopped walking and the buildings of Waterbury rose up out of the misty courtroom and surrounded him again. A woman who was passing laughed. "He said 'Puppy biscuit,'" she said to her companion. "That man said 'Puppy biscuit' to himself." Walter Mitty hurried on. He went into an *A. & P., not the first one he came to but a smaller one farther up the street. "I want some biscuit for small, young dogs," he said to the clerk. "Any special brand, sir?" The greatest pistol shot in the world thought a moment. "It says 'Puppies Bark for It' on the box," said Walter Mitty.

His wife would be through at the hairdresser's in fifteen minutes, Mitty saw in looking at his watch, unless they had trouble drying it; sometimes they had trouble drying it. She didn't like to get to the hotel first; she would want him to be there waiting for her as usual.

He found a big leather chair in the lobby, facing a window, and he put the overshoes and the puppy biscuit on the floor beside it. He picked up an old copy of *Liberty and sank down into the chair. "Can Germany Conquer the World Through the Air?" Walter Mitty looked at the pictures of bombing planes and of ruined streets.

..."The cannonading has *got the wind up in young Raleigh, sir," said the sergeant. Captain Mitty looked up at him through *tousled hair. "Get him to bed," he said wearily. "With the others. I'll fly alone." "But you can't sir," said the sergeant anxiously. "It takes two men to handle that bomber and the *Archies are pounding hell out of the air. *Von Richtman's circus is between here and *Saulier." "Somebody's got to get that ammunition dump," said Mitty. "I'm going over. *Spot of brandy?" He poured a drink for the sergeant and one for himself. War thundered and whined around the *dugout and battered at the door. There was a *rending of wood and splinters flew through the room. "A bit of a near thing," said Captain Mitty carelessly. "The *box barrage is closing in," said the sergeant. "We only live once, Sergeant," said Mitty, with his faint, fleeting smile. "Or do we?" He poured another brandy and *tossed it off. "I never see a man could hold his brandy like you, sir," said the sergeant. "Begging your pardon, sir." Captain Mitty stood up and strapped on his huge Webley-Vickers automatic. "It's forty kilometers through hell, sir," said the sergeant. Mitty finished one last brandy. "After all," he said softly, "what isn't?" The pounding of the cannon increased; there was the rat-tat-tatting of machine guns, and from somewhere came the menacing pocketa-pocketa-pocketa of the new flamethrowers. Walter Mitty walked to the door of the dugout humming *"Auprès de Ma Blonde." He turned and waved to the sergeant. "*Cheerio!" he said....

Something struck his shoulder. "I've been looking all over this hotel for you," said Mrs. Mitty. "Why do you have to hide in this old chair? How did you expect me to find you?" "Things close in," said Walter Mitty vaguely. "What?" Mrs. Mitty said. "Did you get the what's-its-name? The puppy biscuit? What's in that box?" "Overshoes," said Mitty. "Couldn't you have put them on in the store?" "I was thinking," said Walter Mitty. "Does it ever occur to you that I am sometimes thinking?" She looked at him. "I'm going to take your temperature when I get you home," she said.

They went out through the revolving doors that made a faintly *derisive whistling sound when you pushed them. It was two blocks to the parking lot. At the drugstore on the corner she said. " Wait here for me. I forgot something. I won't be a minute." She was more than a minute. Walter Mitty lighted a cigarette. It began to rain, rain with *sleet in it. He stood up against the wall of the drugstore, smoking. . . . He put his shoulders back and his heels together. " To hell with the handkerchief," said Walter Mitty scornfully. He took one last drag on his cigarette and snapped it away. Then, with that faint, fleeting smile playing about his lips, he faced the *firing squad; erect and motionless, proud and *disdainful, Walter Mitty the Undefeated, *inscrutable to the last.

Glossary

A. & P.   The Atlantic and Pacific Tea Company, a large chain of supermarkets

Archie   an anti-aircraft gun (slang)

"Auprès de Ma Blonde"   a jaunty French popular song from World War I; a literal translation of the title is "Next to My Blonde"

bickering   quarreling

box barrage   a heavy screen of artillery fire, here, in a three-dimensional, rectangular (box-shaped) pattern

Cheerio!   good-by (British; colloquial)

crack shot   a person who shoots well

cur   a bad-tempered or worthless dog; here, an insult implying that the man is cowardly and contemptible

derisive   mocking, scoffing

disdainful   contemptuous

District Attorney   the prosecuting officer of an American judical court (the lawyer who argues on behalf of the state)

dugout   a rough covered shelter used by soldiers

firing squad   a group of men charged with executing someone by gun fire

got the wind up   frightened (British; slang)

inscrutable   mysterious, unknowable

insinuatingly   suggesting more than he is saying

let the man have it   hit him (slang)

Liberty   a fictitious popular illustrated magazine

pandemonium   wild and noisy disorder; bedlam

rending   breaking, splintering

Saulier   an imaginary town in France

sleet   falling snow or hail mixed with rain

spot   a small quantity of something (British; colloquial)

tossed it off   drank it in one gulp

tousled   uncombed, disordered

Von Richtman's circus   *Baron Manfred von Richthofen (1892–1918), known as the "Red Baron," was the most famous German military pilot of World War I; he was credited with shooting down more than 80 enemy planes. Walter doesn't get the name quite right in referring to the Baron's flying squadron.*

Webley-Vickers 50.80   a fictitious handgun of fantastic size

Comprehension and Discussion Questions

A. *THE THIRD DAYDREAM*
*1. Where does it take place?

2. Where is Walter Mitty sitting? Who else is in the room?

*3. What causes the "excited buzz"?

4. What question does the District Attorney ask?

5. Why does Mitty's lawyer object to the question?

6. How does Mitty react to his lawyer's interruption?

*7. What events in Mitty's everyday life have made their way into this daydream?

8. How do the people in the courtroom react to Mitty's statement?

*9. What does the District Attorney do when a lovely girl throws herself into Mitty's arms? How does Mitty react?

B. *AWAKE AGAIN*
*1. What makes Walter remember the puppy biscuit?

2. Why does the woman who passes Walter laugh?

*3. Why doesn't Walter go into the first supermarket that he comes to?

4. What kind of dog do the Mittys have?

5. What brand of dog food does Walter buy?

C. *THE FOURTH DAYDREAM*
*1. Where is Walter now? What role has he assumed?

*2. What problem faces him?

*3. Who is with him? Where are the other men?

*4. What is the Sergeant's attitude toward him?

*5. How does Mitty prepare himself for his dangerous mission?

*6. What is his attitude toward the danger?

D. *ONCE MORE AWAKE*
1. What strikes Walter's shoulder?

*2. How does Mrs. Mitty greet her husband?

3. Is she pleased that he has done all the errands she asked him to do?

*4. Why is she going to take Walter's temperature when they get home?

5. How far is the hotel from the parking lot?

*6. Why does Mrs. Mitty ask Walter to wait for her at the drug-store?

7. What kind of weather is it?

E. THE END

*1. How does Walter pass the time while he is waiting for his wife?

*2. Where is he?

*3. What is the crisis this time?

*4. How does he react?

* *These questions are the most important for class discussion.*

Exercises

A. Uses of IT. The pronoun *it* may be used to replace a noun or phrase, refer to the time or weather, or simply act as a grammatical "filler" for the subject position in a sentence. What is the function of *it* in each of the following sentences?

Ex. Toothpaste, toothbrush, bicarbonate, carborundum, initiative and referendum? He gave *it* up.

<u>THE EFFORT TO REMEMBER WHAT HE WAS SUPPOSED TO BUY</u>

1. Mitty let the man have *it* on the point of the chin.

   _____

2. "*It* says 'Puppies Bark for *It*' on the box."

   _____, _____

3. His wife would be through at the hairdresser's in fifteen minutes, unless they had trouble drying *it*.

   _____

4. He found a big leather chair in the lobby, facing a window, and he put the overshoes and the puppy biscuit on the floor beside *it*.

   _____

5. "*It* takes two men to handle that bomber."

    _____

6. He poured another brandy and tossed *it* off.

    _____

7. "*It's* forty kilometers through hell, sir."

    _____

8. "Does *it* ever occur to you that I am sometimes thinking?"

    _____

9. *It* began to rain, rain with sleet in *it*.

    _____, _____

10. He took one last drag on the cigarette and snapped *it* away.

    _____

B. ORDERS. The following commands range from abrupt to rude. Change each one to a more polite form.
Ex. "Not so fast! You're driving too fast."
     PLEASE DON'T DRIVE SO FAST.

1. "Remember to get those overshoes."

    _____

2. "Pick it up, brother!"

    _____

3. "Quiet, man!"

    _____

4. "Give me a fountain pen."

    _____

5. "Get on with the operation."

    _____

6. "Wrong lane, Mac!"

    _____

7. "Hey, brother, better leave the key."

    _____

8. "Don't tell me you forgot the what's-its-name."

    _____

C. SUGGESTIONS. And now change these polite requests or comments to less-polite forms.
Ex. "I wish you'd let Dr. Renshaw look you over."
     I WANT YOU TO LET DR. RENSHAW LOOK YOU OVER.

1. "Why don't you wear your gloves?"
   _____

2. "We can't make it, sir."
   _____

3. "Wish you'd take a look at him."
   _____

4. "If you would take over, Mitty?"
   _____

5. "Any special brand, sir?"
   _____

D. *DRAMATIZATION.* Divide these roles among the members of the class. Scene 5: the DISTRICT ATTORNEY, MITTY'S ATTORNEY, the JUDGE, MITTY, a lovely, dark-haired GIRL. Scene 6: a WOMAN, her COMPANION, WALTER, the CLERK. Scene 7: CAPTAIN MITTY, the SERGEANT. Scene 8: WALTER, MRS. MITTY. Scene 9: WALTER, the FIRING SQUAD, the CAPTAIN of the FIRING SQUAD.

SCENE 5

The District Attorney: Perhaps this will refresh your memory. (*He thrusts a gun at the quiet figure on the witness stand.*) Have you ever seen this before?

Mitty: This is my Webley-Vickers 50.80.
(*An excited buzz runs around the courtroom. The JUDGE raps for order.*)

The D.A.: You are a crack shot with any sort of firearms, I believe?

Mitty's Attorney: Objection! We have shown that the defendant could not have fired the shot. We have shown that he wore his right arm in a sling on the night of the fourteenth of July.

Mitty: (*after silencing the attorneys by raising his hand briefly*) With any known make of gun, I could have killed Gregory Fitzhurst at three hundred feet *with my left hand.*
(*There is pandemonium in the courtroom. A woman's scream rises above the bedlam, and suddenly a lovely dark-haired GIRL is in WALTER MITTY'S arms. The DISTRICT ATTORNEY strikes at her savagely.*)

Mitty: (*Without rising, he hits the D.A. on the point of the chin.*) You miserable cur!

SCENE 6

Walter: Puppy biscuit.

A Woman: (*Laughing as she turns to her* COMPANION) Puppy biscuit. That man said " Puppy biscuit " to himself.

Walter: (*He hurries up the street, going into the second A. & P., which is smaller than the first one he comes to.*) I want some biscuit for small, young dogs.

The Clerk: Any special brand, sir?

Walter: (*after pausing a moment to think*) It says "Puppies Bark for It " on the box. (*He continues to the hotel where he is to meet his wife, settles down in a comfortable chair, and starts to look at an article about German air power in an old magazine.*)

SCENE 7

The Sergeant: The cannonading has got the wind up in young Raleigh, sir.

Captain Mitty: Get him to bed. With the others. I'll fly alone.

The Sergeant: But you can't, sir. It takes two men to handle that bomber and the Archies are pounding hell out of the air. Von Richtman's circus is between here and Saulier.

Captain Mitty: Somebody's got to get that ammunition dump. I'm going over. Spot of brandy? (*A shell lands near by and splinters fly through the door.*) A bit of a near thing.

The Sergeant: The box barrage is closing in.

Captain Mitty: We only live once, Sergeant. Or do we?

The Sergeant: I never see a man could hold his brandy like you, sir. Begging your pardon, sir. ... It's forty kilometers through hell, sir.

Captain Mitty: After all, what isn't? (*He walks out, whistling "Auprès de Ma Blonde."*) Cheerio!

SCENE 8

Mrs. Mitty: I've been looking all over this hotel for you. Why do you have to hide in this old chair? How did you expect me to find you?

Walter: Things close in.

Mrs. Mitty: What? Did you get the what's-its-name? The puppy biscuit? What's in the box?

Walter: Overshoes.

Mrs. Mitty: Couldn't you have put them on in the store?

Walter: I was thinking. Does it ever occur to you that I am sometimes thinking?

Mrs. Mitty: I'm going to take your temperature when I get you home.

> (*They leave the hotel to walk the two blocks to the parking lot. At the corner,* MRS. MITTY *stops.*) Wait here for me. I forgot something. I won't be a minute.

SCENE 9

> (WALTER *lights a cigarette. It begins to rain, rain with sleet in it. He leans against the wall of the drugstore, smoking. The* FIRING SQUAD *line up for the execution. The* CAPTAIN *steps forward to tie a handkerchief over* WALTER'S *eyes.*)

Walter: (*putting his shoulders back and his heels together*) To hell with the handkerchief.

> (*He takes one last drag on his cigarette and snaps it away. Then, with that faint, fleeting smile playing about his lips, he faces the* FIRING SQUAD, *erect and motionless, proud and disdainful,* WALTER MITTY, *the Undefeated, inscrutable to the last.*)

Biographical Notes on the Authors
and
Suggestions for Further Reading

JOHN COLLIER (1901-   )

English by birth, John Collier has spent his recent years in Los Angeles and is frequently published in American magazines. He has written poetry and novels, but is best known for his short stories, which often have an odd, ironic twist with a touch of the supernatural.

"The Chaser" is from *Fancies and Goodnights* (1951). Other collections of Collier's work include *A Touch of Nutmeg* (1945) and *The John Collier Reader* (1972).

ERNEST HEMINGWAY (1899-1961)

Hemingway was born in Oak Park, Illinois, a Chicago suburb and the kind of town where "The Killers" might have been set. His wide travels and adventurous life provided the background for his many short stories and novels. Perhaps his most famous short story is "The Snows of Kilamanjaro," set in Africa. His most celebrated novels are *The Sun Also Rises* (1926), set in Paris and northern Spain; *A Farewell to Arms* (1929), set in Italy during World War I; *For Whom the Bell Tolls* (1940), about the Spanish Civil War; and *The Old Man and the Sea* (1952), set in Cuba, for which Hemingway won the Nobel and Pulitzer prizes for literature.

Hemingway is famous for his lean style, which has been widely imitated but never matched. His heros all show physical courage in the face of danger, a characteristic which Hemingway admired greatly and which he prided himself on possessing. Unwilling to live with the inevitable physical deterioration of old age, Hemingway committed suicide, as his father, a physician, had done before him under similar circumstances.

SHIRLEY JACKSON (1919-1965)

Miss Jackson was born in San Francisco and spent her youth in California. In *Life Among the Savages* (1953) and *Raising Demons* (1956), she humorously described life in North Bennington, Vermont with her husband, the literary critic Stanley Edgar Hyman, and their four children. She died quietly of heart failure at the age of 46.

A prolific writer, Miss Jackson was a regular contributor to *The New Yorker* for ten years. "The Lottery" first appeared in that magazine and has subsequently been reprinted in numerous anthologies, and has been dramatized for radio and television. Miss Jackson's husband reports that "She was always proud that the Union of South Africa banned 'The Lottery' and she felt that *they* at least understood the story."*

She is best known for her stories and novels in the genre known as "Gothic," which typically involves a seemingly-innocent heroine who is nonetheless implicated in at least one violent death, often that of a close relative. The atmosphere is always one of horror and mystery in the midst of genteel surroundings and, as in Collier's work, there are often supernatural elements. Miss Jackson's highly successful novel *We Have Always Lived in the Castle* (1962) exemplifies this style.

JESSE STUART (1907-

The son of an illiterate tenant farmer from eastern Kentucky, Jesse Stuart had little formal education as a child. When he finally managed to attend high school, and then college, he discovered that he had a talent for writing. He has pursued a successful career as a writer, at the same time serving as a teacher and administrator in southern schools.

In addition to short stories, Stuart has written poetry, novels, an autobiography (*The Thread that Runs So True*, 1958) and a bio-

---

* Stanley Edgar Hyman in the Preface to *The Magic of Shirley Jackson* p. viii, New York: Farrar, Straus and Giroux, Inc., 1966

graphy of his father (*God's Oddling*, 1960). It was from his father that the author gained his great love of nature and appreciation of individuality. And it was almost certainly from his father that the idea for "Love" came, for in *God's Oddling* Stuart records,

> "A blacksnake is a pretty thing," he once said to me, "so shiny and black in the spring sun after he sheds his winter skin."
> He was the first man I ever heard say a snake was pretty. I never forgot his saying it. I can even remember the sumac thicket where he saw the blacksnake.*

JAMES THURBER (1894-1961)

After spending his boyhood and university days in Columbus, Ohio, Thurber worked as a reporter, serving for a time as a foreign correspondent in France. He was one of the young, talented writers— E. B. White was another—recruited when Harold Ross founded *The New Yorker* in 1925, a period recounted in Thurber's best-selling *My Years with Ross* (1959).

Thurber subsequently devoted full time to writing and illustrating some two dozen books of stories and essays. He collaborated with Elliott Nugent in writing a play, *The Male Animal*, which ran successfully in New York in 1940. Several of Thurber's stories and sketches were also presented on Broadway in *Three by Thurber* (1955) and *A Thurber Carnival* (1960). A number of his stories, including "The Unicorn in the Garden" and "The Secret Life of Walter Mitty" (with Walter played by Danny Kaye) have been produced as movies.

A representative selection of Thurber's short stories, fables, essays and cartoons is available in *The Thurber Carnival* (1945). His wide-eyed dogs, predatory women, and timid men have made him one of America's best-loved humorists.

---

* Jesse Stuart in *God's Oddling*, excerpted in *A Jesse Stuart Reader*, New York: McGraw-Hill, 1963.

JOHN UPDIKE (1932-   )

Updike was born in a small town in western Pennsylvania, where his father taught school, having previously been a telephone cable-splicer (cf. " a telephone lineman " among the orphaned swimming pool's assorted users). After graduating from Harvard, John Updike spent a year at Oxford and then joined *The New Yorker* as a staff writer, following in the steps of Thurber and White. Indeed he has cited Thurber as one of his first " literary idols." He left the magazine in 1957 to devote all his time to writing serious fiction.

One of the most successful contemporary American writers, Updike is a perfectionist, a master of both technique and style. His short stories, humorous poems, and essays appear regularly and he has published a number of novels, among them *Rabbit, Run* (1960), perhaps his best work, and *The Centaur* (1963), which won the National Book Award for fiction. His short stories have been collected in several volumes, among them *Pigeon Feathers* (1962) and *Museums and Women* (1972), from which "The Orphaned Swimming Pool" is taken.

E. B. WHITE (1899-   )

Elwyn Brooks White was born in Mt. Vernon, New York, attended Cornell University, and then worked as a journalist and editorial writer in New York City. At the age of 40, he moved to a farm in Maine, from which he has pursued a distinguished literary career.

White's humorous essays and anecdotes have been collected in *One Man's Meat* (1944), *The Second Tree from the Corner* (1954)—from which "The Hour of Letdown" is taken, and *The Points of My Compass* (1962). His published writings also include two volumes of poetry and three children's classics—*Stuart Little* (1945), *Charlotte's Web* (1952), and *The Trumpet of the Swan* (1970).

White and Thurber collaborated on *Is Sex Necessary?*, a satire on pseudo-scientific sex literature, in 1929. With his wife, Katherine, White edited *A Subtreasury of American Humor* (1941). His revised edition of *The Elements of Style*, a composition handbook originally written by White's Cornell English professor William Strunk, Jr. was a surprise best-seller when it appeared in 1959. And its wit, charm and usefulness have made it a continuing favorite of those interested in the craft of prose writing.

WILLIAM CARLOS WILLIAMS (1883-1963)

The son of immigrants—his father was English, his mother Puerto Rican—Williams was born in Rutherford, New Jersey. He attended preparatory schools in New York and Switzerland, graduated from the University of Pennsylvania Medical School, and studied pediatrics in Leipzig, Germany.

For 40 years, Williams practiced medicine in Rutherford, specializing in the care of infants and children. At the same time, he was one of the most prolific twentieth-century American authors, publishing his first volume of poems at the age of 23. In all he has written 600 poems, 52 short stories, four novels, an opera libretto, history, essays, biography and an autobiography, *Autobiography of William Carlos Williams* (1951).

In his poetry, as in "The Use of Force," Williams writes of familiar objects and events—a daisy, a wheelbarrow, a funeral—using them as the basis for philosophical speculation. His work is included in all the standard anthologies of modern American poetry.